FORGED IN MAGIC

IN MAGIC
BOOK SIX

KJ WARAWA

MYSTIC
CITY
PRESS

Edited by Jennia D'Lima

Proofread by Taylor Gonzales

Cover Designed by Sunset Rose Books

Hey there,

If you're wondering what happened to Sam after she was rescued in *Found in Magic* and Mirek and Rocky after they were rescued in *Love in Magic*… stay tuned. You'll get a peek at Sam and Mirek in *Forged in Magic* before they get their happy ever after in the last book in the series, *Forever in Magic*.

The three final books in the series take place almost at the same time. The final part of *Love in Magic* (Reece and Isabella) overlaps with the beginning of *Forged in Magic* (Kate and Isaac) and that story takes place at the same time as *Forever in Magic* (Sam and Mirek). When you read them in order, it will all make sense—I promise!

Did you notice I didn't mention Rocky? He's definitely a tortured soul after taking the wrong path as a teenager and not knowing how to make things right. He deserves his own happy ever after, and he'll get one... just not yet. Right now, it's Kate and Isaac's turn, so it's time to see how they'll survive what's coming their way...

Happy Reading!
    KJ

Kate Stone shivered from the early November cold as she watched her non-magic client drive away before she flashed inside her blacksmith shop. The Stone Forge was her pride and joy, something that would never let her down. Unlike a man.

Isaac had asked her to come over tonight. Her body didn't have a problem with it because he could bring it to life like matches to dry kindling. It was her brain and her heart that were putting up some resistance.

If she could just convince Isaac to fuck her and nothing else, then she'd be good. When she first saw him, it had been lust at first sight. He was tall with a lean musculature, a handsome face, and although his arms had been covered, she'd soon learned he had tattoos. Win, win, win in her book.

Part of the attraction could have been that Isaac Hull not only had tattoos, but that he also inked them on others. He was magic like her, as were all her friends and family, but he had a rare magic ability. Isaac could sense emotions when he touched people, and it allowed him to embed magical properties into the tattoos he inked. Not only was his specialty similar to hers, they were also both artists. And while she worked with metal, he worked with ink—making him even more irresistible.

When he first came to Blue Mountain, Colorado, the city she claimed as home, their arrangement was only supposed to be temporary. She thought she could fuck him and move on because he lived in another city. Then Isaac decided to stay.

Since the chemistry between them had been off the charts, they were both willing to indulge. And often. Living in the same city became a problem when they started to see each other all the time. As time went on Isaac wanted more than just sex—the exact thing she'd been hoping to avoid.

Tonight, he was going to cook her dinner. Or maybe conjure dinner—same thing. That would lead to conversation while they ate and getting to know each other better. From there, it would progress to sleepovers. Kate wasn't one to turn her nose up at morning sex—it was the cozy breakfast that followed because that could lead to him thinking they were a couple. As soon as that happened, he would want more from her, or want her to change, and that's when she'd get hurt.

Isaac was already starting to make her want more. He made her feel special, and at odd times of the day, she often wondered what he was doing or if she should pop into his shop to see how he was doing.

It was a dangerous path to go down. Maybe it had been too long since she'd given herself a reminder why going that route led to hurt. But she had a simple remedy for that.

She walked over to the small desk off to the side of her workbench and pulled out the letter-size envelope tucked into the drawer. Using her magic, she got rid of the dust, opened the flap, and dumped the contents onto the desk.

As the years passed, the pain brought on by seeing each item lessened. It was seeing them all together that hurt so much—a reminder that she had been burnt more than once, and if she didn't remember that, it could happen again.

As she did every time, Kate picked up the ribbon first. She let the green silk slide through her fingers and remembered how excited she'd been when the hair stylist had weaved it into her up-do. She and her friends had been talking about prom their entire senior year, and Kate had hung her dress and hair ribbon on her closet door for months in anticipation.

Brandon had been a friend of her brother's in college. When he'd asked a few days before the dance to take her to prom, she'd been over the moon.

The euphoria had lasted right up until the moment Brandon left her to dance with her friend Sonya. After their third dance, Brandon and Sonya stopped for a drink and he took Kate aside. He confessed to his real reason for asking Kate to the prom. Brandon had been infatuated with Sonya ever since he'd seen her when he had been at the house with Damon. All he'd needed was a way to meet her that would seem casual and friendly. Kate was that way.

Kate put the ribbon back in the envelope and picked up one of the pieces of the credit card she had cut up.

Holding it in her fist, she closed her eyes and pictured Justin, who had been her boyfriend for six months. She had been so sure she was in love with him. Right up until the day he stood in front of her and said the betting had just gotten a bit out of hand, and he had been so sure the last one was going to make him rich. It wasn't his fault that someone gave him bad advice.

If Kate had truly loved him, a measly twenty-thousand dollars should have been nothing, he'd said. He had needed a fast way to get cash to pay off his loan shark, or the guy's enforcers would have hurt him. Kate should understand, he'd said, since one of the only things magic people couldn't conjure was dollar bills due to them being counterfeit. Justin accused her of being a cold-hearted bitch, saying that all she cared about was the debt he'd racked up on her credit cards and not him.

Kate picked up the credit card pieces one at a time and put them back in the envelope. Then she picked up the last reminder—a drawing of a sword—and put it in the envelope with the ribbon and credit card pieces. She didn't need to relive what had happened with the drawing because the pain and humiliation Ethan had caused was always with her.

Ethan and the others had shown her that love and trust were nothing more than a myth. "Nope, never again. Sex or nothing," she muttered, the motto she'd adopted five years ago to protect her heart.

After putting the envelope back in the desk, she looked at the clock on the wall. Still over an hour before she had to be at Isaac's. With her motto fresh in her mind, she'd be able to keep it to only sex.

Maybe if she went now, he wouldn't be ready for

dinner, and they could just have sex. Then she'd be sated and could leave.

Liking her plan, she used her magic to lock her shop and put a small protection spell on the building. If Maverick really wanted to get into her shop, the spell wouldn't stop him, but it might deter one of his minions. She didn't know how much evil magic Maverick possessed, but just knowing he currently used it to terrorize all magics made her extra careful.

With one final glance at her shop, she flashed to Isaac's apartment.

Kate always went to his place, even though she loved her two-story Craftsman-style house sitting on the same two acres where she'd built her workshop. Coming to Isaac's meant she could leave whenever she wanted. Just like she would today.

Kate touched down in the hallway outside Isaac's door. Not bothering to knock, she entered his apartment. She didn't see or hear Isaac in the bright and airy open concept space.

As she walked down the hallway toward the bedrooms, she listened for where he might be, although the place only had two bedrooms.

When she heard the shower running, her excitement amped up. Slowing her pace, she used her magic to get rid of her clothes because they would only get in the way. Knowing she wouldn't need them later, she magically sent them home. Her hair tie was gone too, her red hair flowing down her back and hitting just above her ass.

Now completely naked, she stepped into Isaac's bedroom. The door to his bathroom was wide open. Leaning against the doorframe, she took in the sight of water sluicing down over six-feet-two inches of tattooed lean muscle. Isaac had almost two full sleeves—his arms were both covered in black and gray designs. Kate loved watching Isaac's muscles ripple under the ink whenever he gripped her hips and thrust into her.

When Isaac reached for the shampoo on the shower stall's shelf, he turned enough to give Kate a glimpse of the owl inked on his chest. She'd enjoyed licking every inch of that piece of art. More than once.

Never before had she been as attracted to a man as she was to Isaac. Even Ethan hadn't been the visual delight that Isaac was. Just watching him had her wet and ready for him. That's why she had to remember her motto and guard her heart.

Enough watching.

Kate walked up to the large shower stall and pulled open the glass door. Isaac turned, his light-gray eyes widening when she walked into the steam-filled enclosure and closed the door behind her.

"Hey, beautiful. Didn't have a chance to shower at home?" he teased, his deep voice sending a thrill to her lady parts.

"Something like that."

Isaac raised an eyebrow at her cryptic comment, but lust that matched her own was evident in his eyes.

With just a look, he could make her feel like the most beautiful woman on the planet. Most people would think that was a good thing. She supposed it was, but if she wasn't careful, it could lead to those pesky relationship feelings she needed to avoid.

Not wanting to ruin the moment with unwanted thoughts, she took a step forward and wound her arms around his neck. The warm water soaked her hair down her back as she went up onto her toes.

Each time their lips met, she felt the same excitement as she had the very first time they'd kissed. During the months they'd been together, she kept waiting for the feeling to wane. But it never did.

Her kiss wasn't gentle, but Isaac always gave as good as he got, and the rough passion lit something inside her. They plundered each other's mouths as their hands roamed over one another's bodies.

When he gripped her hips with both hands, he lifted her enough so she could feel the solid, hard length of his cock against her stomach. Her fingernails bit into his shoulders; she wasn't sure which one of them groaned. "Yes! Fuck. More," she grunted as he held her in the air. Rubbing against him, she tried to create the friction she so desperately craved.

"More what, baby?" His voice was deep and raspy as his lips moved from her mouth down along her neck. Her feet landed on the wet tile as he lowered her, then his mouth and hands worked their way south, lighting her up like a forge turned on high.

She gripped his shoulders, then moved her fingers into his hair. The sounds he made when she tugged on the wet strands told her he didn't want a gentle touch either.

Her breath caught in her throat as he took one of her nipples into his mouth, sucking hard. At the same time, he used his hand to knead her other breast.

"This what you want?" he asked as he switched to her other side, taking her nipple lightly between his teeth.

"You. I want—" His hands and mouth on her heated

skin were such a distraction, her thoughts fled, like they were swept away in a strong wind.

She was becoming wetter by the second, and it had nothing to do with the water raining down on them. An ache had formed in her core, and she desperately needed Isaac to soothe it. The fact that he was the only one she ever wanted to take care of that problem was becoming an issue. Something she would have to think about later, not when every nerve in her body had awakened, waiting for his touch.

Isaac overwhelmed all her senses.

He trailed one of his hands down her stomach to her core, and when he slipped a finger between her wet folds, she bucked against him. Another groan escaped her as she pushed against his hand. "Oh, fuck... yes. More."

"You haven't answered me." He pulled his fingers away, and she looked down where he was now kneeling before her, the water streaming down his back. "What is it you want, Kate? I need you to tell me."

"Fuck. I need you to fuck me."

"You don't want my mouth on you? Right here?" His fingers teased at her lower lips, and she arched into them, needing him more than she wanted to admit.

Kate loved a great round of oral sex. What woman didn't? But it was more intimate than sex. Even with her recent reminders, she was too vulnerable for that tonight.

She gripped his shoulders and pulled him up. "Please, Isaac. I need you to fuck me. Now!"

He kissed her mouth and nipped her bottom lip. "Impatient."

"Please—" If begging was what it took, she was willing

to do it, but when he gripped her ass and lifted her against him, she didn't have to.

She wrapped her legs around him and fell forward against his chest as he leaned back against the glass wall.

One of his hands cradled her ass more fully. He used his magic to support her to free his other hand. He wouldn't get a complaint from her.

Then all thoughts fled once again, and only sensation remained as he eased her down onto his cock. They'd done away with condoms months ago. Thank fuck.

He filled her completely, and she felt a sudden sense of everything being right, like she'd needed Isaac to make her feel complete. She wished she could bottle the feeling to enjoy it anytime she wanted.

"Unwrap your legs," he demanded against her neck, where his tongue was doing delicious things to her. Doing as he'd directed, she pulled her legs from around him and let them fall to his sides. His back was fully flush against the glass now, giving him more balance as he bent his knees.

Then he gave her exactly what she craved. His hands tightened on her hips as he thrust up into her, over and over. She felt a pocket of air under her ass and loved the assistance of his magic. Knowing she could let go of her death grip on his shoulders, she cupped his face in both hands and kissed him with all the passion building inside her.

Isaac set a punishing pace as he plunged into her, shortening his thrusts. Their breathing picked up. "Yes! Isaac!" she yelled as her body tightened and an orgasm came barreling at her. Pleasure rocked through her entire core, more intense than she'd ever felt before.

Still punching up into her, Isaac forced another orgasm from her, her body spasming with aftershocks as he yelled her name and went over the peak with her.

When Kate's breathing slowed down, she noticed the water had become tepid, cooling off her heated skin. Isaac pulled out of her and lowered her feet to the ground. As he did, he kissed her softly on the lips. "That was unexpected and amazing. After dinner, I'd like to spend more time showing you my appreciation."

Kate felt unsteady on her feet, still reeling from the orgasms that had rocked her world, as she looked up at Isaac. She thought she saw something in his eyes that looked a lot like love. A cold panic coursed through her as she wondered if he would see the same thing reflected back at him in her eyes.

"I… I can't… I came to tell you I can't stay for dinner." Not wanting to see the disappointment on Isaac's face, she flashed home.

She landed in her living room, dripping wet. Using her magic, she dried herself off as she walked naked to her bedroom. She had told Isaac over and over again that all she wanted from him was sex. Yet why did she suddenly feel a deep sense of loss and shame from high-tailing it out of his shower after getting exactly what she'd asked for?

"THANK YOU," Isaac said, leaning back to give the server room to remove his plate from the table. Isaac looked across the table at Meredith, who had invited him to lunch at The Magic Plate. She had called it a combined business slash family lunch.

Setting up his shop in one of their buildings had worked out better than he'd originally thought, and it was one of the things Meredith had wanted to talk about. There was a lot of craziness going on with magics and she said she was checking in with everyone. And since they both needed to eat lunch, they could do that and catch up. Her husband Jack, an old friend of Isaac's, had joined them.

The Williams family had folded Isaac into their arms, and he was grateful for it. His mom was his only remaining family member, and he didn't see her often, but the Williams made him feel like he'd gained a hoard of brothers and sisters.

That made him think of how he met Kate. He definitely didn't think of her as a sister or a cousin. More like a girlfriend who drove him crazy. She had flashed out of his shower over a week ago and had been ghosting him since then—something he was ready to remedy.

"How's your meal?" Meredith asked. All three of them had dug right in with very little talk. Everything at The Magic Plate was too delicious to resist when it was fresh and piping hot.

"Great, as always. How have the staff been with—" Isaac cut himself off when Jack raised his hand. By the look of concentration on his face, he was receiving a telepathic message. Since Jack and Meredith had the power to receive and send messages over long distances, the message could be coming from anywhere.

"That was Reece," Jack said as he stood. "Kate was attacked."

Isaac stood and followed Jack and Meredith. It surprised him that his legs could even carry him since he wouldn't have been able to speak if asked. Jack's words had frozen Isaac with fear, sending chills throughout his body. Only by sheer force of will was he able to move.

They walked into a back hallway they used to flash in and out of. Without a word, they each flashed to the entrance of Kate's workshop.

Reece and Isabella stood in the middle of the large space. When Isaac saw Kate on the ground, his legs threatened to give out again. Even though she had been keeping her distance from him, it wasn't what he wanted, and this time, he was going to be there for her, whether she wanted him to or not. With his heart in his throat, he flashed to her side.

"We're here," Jack said, alerting Reece and Isabella as Isaac, Meredith, and Jack walked up behind them.

"What happened?" Isaac asked as he knelt by Kate's head. He had to force himself not to panic when he saw blood on her forehead. Floating his hand over the injured area, he used his magic to heal the cut, and any trace it was ever there disappeared.

"We don't know," Reece said. "When we got here, we noticed one of the doors was off its hinges and put out some feelers but didn't sense anyone inside."

Jack hovered his hands over Kate's torso. "Bruises and a hit to the head, but I've healed her. She'll be fine," Jack said as he waved his hand over Kate one more time.

Thankful that Jack was able to heal Kate, Isaac waited for Kate to wake up as he expected that was the aim of Jack's final gesture.

Kate moaned and her eyes flung open. "Wha—" She

struggled to sit up, but Isaac reached for her before she could. Sitting on the floor behind her, he pulled her up so she could lean against him and then waited for her to protest. It didn't matter what she said; he didn't want to let her go.

"I'm fine." Kate batted one of Isaac's hands away and pushed herself forward to sit up before wobbling backward.

Isaac pulled her higher onto his lap, his arms around her waist. "For Christ's sake, woman. You were unconscious; give yourself a second." He'd kept his voice low, and she only hesitated a second before settling back against him. Isaac wanted to run his hands over every inch of her to make sure Jack hadn't missed anything, but he refrained. Kate would hate him fussing over her. Not that he would consider making sure she was okay fussing, but she would.

"Kate, can you tell us how you got hurt?" Meredith asked.

"Someone came up behind me. I was using my power hammer, so it was too loud. I didn't notice anyone was there until someone grabbed my arm. When they spun me around, I used my magic to grab a blade, and I jabbed at the guy but missed. It was like he had superspeed."

"You should have flashed away," Isaac said close to Kate's ear. He knew she was tough, but she didn't have to constantly try to prove it.

"Flash away? Are you crazy?" Kate's voice rose an octave as she twisted in his arms to glare at him. "My forge is my life! I wasn't going to leave all my equipment and let a bunch of assholes do whatever they wanted! And what about the mirrors? Did you just want me to leave them too?"

"No, of course not," Isaac said, not able to hold back the sarcasm. "But instead, you let them almost take your actual life!" He wasn't sure whether he wanted to hold her tighter to protect her or knock the damn chip off her shoulder. Maybe both.

"Why are you here, anyway?" Kate asked as if he'd been waiting around just to flash to her.

"I was having lunch with Jack and Meredith when Reece messaged Jack."

"You didn't have to come," Kate said again.

"What? You think—"

"Kate," Jack said, putting a halt to what Isaac was about to say next, which was probably a good thing. The first time Isaac saw her in over a week and she'd been hurt, which didn't sit well with him. Though anytime she was hurt didn't sit well. "Tell us the rest," Jack prompted.

Kate turned around, her back settling against Isaac's chest, and he wrapped his arms around her again. "There were three of them. The guy who grabbed me, a woman, and another guy. The third guy didn't come near me, but he was definitely the one in charge."

"What did he look like?" Isabella asked.

"The boss guy? His head was almost shaved, and he had olive-toned skin. The backs of his hands were covered in tattoos, but I couldn't make any of them out."

Some of the color drained from Isabella's face. "Eddie. He's my brother. Reece and I have already had a couple of run-ins with him. Was he looking for the mirrors?"

"Oh, shit. I don't know if they got them!" Kate struggled again to get up, but Isaac didn't want to loosen his hold on her. "Kate—" he said quietly in her ear.

"I'll check," Jack said as he stood and walked to the back of the workshop.

Isaac looked over at Jack as he pulled on the locker door and swung it open. The locker was empty. Kate was going to blame herself, even though she had been caught by surprise and outnumbered. He still hadn't figured out how she'd gotten the chip on her shoulder, but she seemed determined to prove something to someone.

"The door was still locked, but someone dissolved the spell," Jack said as he walked back over. "Only someone with Maverick's magic could have destroyed the spell I cast. Which means that the spells we're using on the buildings at night aren't going to be enough to keep out Maverick and his people."

Meredith grasped her husband's hand. "Plus, we still have to figure out how to close the magic box since the mirrors didn't work."

"We found the answer!" Isabella said, her voice full of excitement. All eyes turned to her. "It wasn't the metal frames we needed to find. It's the mirrors!"

Reece dropped his arms from around Isabella and stepped forward. "We'll get the mirrors back. We know where Eddie hangs out."

"What help do you need?" Jack asked.

"Some kind of backup, but I don't know yet. Isabella and I should go in first since Eddie will be expecting us."

Jack furrowed his brows. "Then you'll need more people."

Isaac watched the interchange as Reece and Jack made plans, but he wasn't really listening. Part of him was still focused on Kate. Running his hands up and down her arms, he could feel her tension, but he purposely avoided activating his magic to sense her essence. Out of respect for her, he wouldn't do it unless she asked. But even without using his special ability to feel emotions, he could sense her decreasing adrenaline.

When everyone agreed to go back to The Magic Plate for a late lunch, Isaac bowed out for himself and Kate. Sensing a growing feeling of shame welling up within her, Isaac prepared himself.

2

he second the last person flashed away, Kate jumped to her feet and spun to face Isaac. She hadn't wanted to make a scene while the others were around, but now that they were gone, she could let all her feelings out on Isaac.

Hands on her hips, Kate stared him down where he was still sitting on the ground. "How dare you come barging in here like—"

"Like someone who cares about you? Like someone who was worried because you were attacked?" he drawled as he slowly got to his feet.

"Yes…! No…! That's not what I meant." Fuck. Isaac had the ability to confuse the hell out of her. Ever since she had flashed out of his place, naked as the day she was born, she'd been fighting with herself. During seven long sleepless nights, she had reminded herself why she only wanted sex. Why she *should* only want sex. Anything more was too dangerous. She'd already had her heart ripped more than once. When you loved someone, you were vulnerable. And when you were vulnerable, they knew just how to hurt you the most.

"What *do* you mean, Kate?" Isaac asked softly.

She hated that he always used her name—it made conversations seem too intimate. Like he was giving her his undivided attention and no one else mattered. He was so hard to resist when he did that. And she needed to resist him because if she didn't, she'd start to develop feelings.

She worried that maybe it was already too late—that she did care. When he had charged in earlier and pulled her back against his chest, she had felt protected, and the horrors of the attack started to recede.

"I meant…" She let her words trail off because he was right. He had charged into her shop like someone who cared, and that had scared the shit out of her. But as soon as she finally let him in, he would do something to hurt her, just like all the others had.

During last week's sleepless nights, she had wondered how Isaac had felt when she disappeared. Each time he had texted and she ignored his message, she felt ashamed for dismissing him, but she couldn't make herself reply either. Texting back would have sent mixed signals. He for sure would have then thought she cared about him. So she worked to shove all those pesky relationship feelings down deep where she couldn't acknowledge them. But no matter how deep she pushed them they kept popping back up.

Isaac took another step forward and Kate backed up. Neither of them said a word as they both continued their dance—him forward and her retreating, until her back was against the locker and she had nowhere else to go. Sure, she could flash to the other side of her shop, but then he would think his nearness was getting to her.

It wasn't. She would stand her ground.

Isaac put his hands on the locker on either side of her and leaned his head near hers. They weren't touching, but he was so close. She could feel his warm breath against her cheek. "I know why you left last week and why you're pulling away now," he whispered.

If she looked up, her lips would be close enough to touch his. Something she'd been craving since she'd left him standing in his shower. Instead, she kept her gaze on his shirt and tried not to look at the owl's wing peeking out of the top of his shirt like a sexy invitation. "Why?"

"You're a coward, Kate."

"What?" She shoved at his chest with both hands. Without using magic, she wouldn't have had a chance of budging him, not if he hadn't wanted her to. She was thankful for the space when he moved back, but hurt he called her a coward. For her entire adult life, she'd been brave and had stood up for herself because she'd been the lone female in a man's world.

Many a time she'd been naïve and even fearful, but not once had she been a coward. Self-preservation was not cowardice; protecting her heart from being broken took bravery.

"Yes, a coward." Isaac's deep, raspy voice always got to her, and when she looked up at him, ready to fight again, the look in his eyes knocked the air from her lungs. "You're running because you're scared to feel. I came because I was worried about you. I care for you, Kate, and I know you care for me too. I won't let you push me away, and I will do everything in my power to never hurt you."

She had the sudden urge to melt into him. To bask in everything he was offering. To forget that he had the ability to hurt her and rip her world into shreds. If only it was that easy—just forget what could happen and let him care for her. Maybe even love her. But then what? What would happen when he wanted more from her? When he wanted to use her for his own gain?

Straightening her shoulders, she looked him in the eyes. "You're wrong. I'm not a coward; I just know what I want. I told you from the beginning that I only want sex from you. Are you going to give me sex? Because if you're not, you don't have anything else to give me." Her gaze didn't waver from his, but she hoped deep in her soul that she was telling the truth.

In the next instant, she found herself tugged snugly against Isaac's hard body. She was stiff at first, but then the scent of him—strong and masculine—seeped into her and she was powerless to resist him.

Melting against him, she felt her heart rate finally slowing down.

For the first time since the attack, she closed her eyes, and the events of the attack played like a movie in her mind.

She flung her eyes back open, and yet she could still see the hard gleam in the stranger's eyes as he directed his minions to hurt her. Not just some guy—Isabella's brother. That knowledge almost made it worse—such a despicable person related to someone who had become her friend in the short time they'd known each other.

A shudder rippled through her from head to toe, and then she felt a soothing heat from Isaac's hands as they roamed across her back.

Needing to get herself back on solid ground, she pushed against his chest.

"Oh no, you don't," Isaac said, pulling her back into his arms. "I told you, I'll never intentionally hurt you. I've got you."

Kate stiffened, even though she wanted nothing more than to let herself go slack and allow him to take all her weight. The weight of not just her body but of everything she felt as well. The pressure to be strong and keep her distance from caring. The anxiety from the attack.

"Shhh," Isaac whispered against her hair. "You don't have to be strong all the time, Kate."

His words were like a splash of cold water on her face.

Pulling from his embrace, she took a step back. "*I am* strong. And you have to make up your mind. Am I strong or am I a coward? You can't have it both ways, Isaac."

Isaac barked a harsh sound she wasn't sure she had ever heard from him before. "That's where you're wrong, Kate. You can be strong and still lean on the people who care about you when you need to. But what you're doing right now isn't strong. You're running away from your feelings, and that's what cowards do. And that's what I'm trying to tell you. You're strong inside, but you fight your feelings by running. Instead of running, lean on me." By the time Isaac finished talking, his breathing sounded harsh in the quiet room.

Kate didn't think hers was any quieter. She could feel her heart pounding like it wanted to beat out of her chest. Her experiences had taught her that Isaac was wrong.

"Self-preservation is not running. I'm protecting myself and that is strong and brave." She would have to remember to add that to her other motto of "sex or nothing."

"I don't need to lean on you, and I don't need you to care about me or come running to save me." She steeled herself for his response when she made her next statement. "All I'm willing to offer you is sex. Take it or leave it."

Isaac faced Kate, her shoulders tense and rigid as if she was steeling herself to accept his rejection.

No matter what she said, he knew she was running scared and that the only time she let herself feel when she was around him was during sex. Self-preservation or not, she was still running and that was cowardly. But he understood. He'd done his own fair share of running over the years. Even moving to Blue Mountain so he no longer had to deal with his past had been because he was running.

When he had flashed into her workshop and saw her lying on the ground, it was like he was reliving his worst nightmare. A feeling of being cold had instantly swamped him, threatening to send him down a dark mental path. Only by forcing himself to focus on his surroundings did he manage to stay in the moment and not let his mind take him back to another tragic time.

When he'd managed to move forward, Kate had been his only concern. He hadn't spoken to her since she'd flashed out of his bathroom, but he understood why. She feared her feelings, and he knew he had to let her come to terms with them. It was why he had texted and called but hadn't gone to her house to confront her.

If he hadn't been with Jack and Meredith to hear about Kate's attack, he would have eventually heard about it from someone. Then, no matter how much he wanted to give her space, he would have sought her out to make sure she was okay.

Since she was physically unharmed, he wanted her to see that what she was doing was running. But he wouldn't. She wasn't ready to face it and forcing the issue might make her push him away for good. He was a patient man and Kate needed every ounce of patience he possessed.

If Kate truly only wanted sex, he was willing to give it to her, but it would be on his terms. "Sex or nothing, huh? That's all you're offering?"

As much as Kate tried to project bravado, he could see the fear in her eyes that he was going to reject her.

That wasn't going to happen. Not today. Likely not ever. He cared for her deeply, and although he wasn't sure yet if it was love, he was all for trying to figure it out.

"I accept," he said. For now. He would take his time to convince her they deserved more than just sex and would be good together. She was worth it.

"What?"

Her eyes were so large with surprise, he had to force his features to stay neutral and not smile.

"I said I accept your offer of sex or nothing. Come here."

"Now?"

"Sure. Why not?" He loved keeping her on her proverbial toes. It would ensure things never got boring between them. "You don't want sex right now?"

He saw the exact moment she realized she'd walked into his trap and that the usual chip on her shoulder had settled back into place. It may have even grown an inch or two. If she refused him, her entire speech would have been a lie, and she might have to admit to caring about him.

"I… yeah… sure. Sex now would be great."

Never for a moment did he think she would walk away from his challenge, but now he had to follow through. Looking over at her workbench, he came up with the perfect plan. Taking her hand, he guided her the several feet to the bench.

"What are you doing? I have a nice couch at my house."

She hadn't offered her bed, only the couch, because it was one more way she tried to distance herself. A couch wasn't intimate—not like a bed. At least, that's what he was sure she thought, just like her going to his place would keep her in control, but he'd caught onto her months ago. He would have loved to take her up on her offer of going to her house since they never met there, but he had a plan. Kate wasn't going to control the situation this time.

Waving his hand at the bench, he conjured a thick blanket, ensuring it was smooth and big enough to cover the surface. Then he gripped Kate by the hips and lifted her so she was sitting on the bench. He stood between her legs, her knees touching his hips.

"Ah, a little difficult to have sex on my bench. Especially since I have clothes on."

He directed a smirk her way and then waved his hand again, but this time, he used his magic to remove her worn jeans she wore for work, and then her panties. Her clothes lay folded on the bench beside her.

She laughed at him, and after the last hour, the sound was music to his ears. "You missed something. You have to get rid of your clothes too."

"Nope, not today." He leaned in and kissed her. Not in a rush, he kept the kiss soft and gentle. But he knew if he lingered too long, she would try to speed things up because to Kate, soft and gentle meant caring, which could lead to being hurt, and fast and rushed meant just sex. She was wrong, but she also wasn't ready to learn that yet.

As he continued to kiss her, he dragged the fingers on one hand down her body, skimming them along her skin. When she shivered, he wasn't sure whether it was from excitement or the November chill seeping into her shop.

He pushed his magic into his fingers, warming them as they continued their downward journey.

"Oh my god," she said against his lips. "Your fingers feel so good."

Cradling the back of her neck with one hand so he could continue to kiss her, he moved his other between her legs. She was wet and ready for him. Starting with one finger, he began fucking her. He had to hold onto his plan to only give and not take from her at the moment because he wished it was his dick surrounded by her tight warmth and not his fingers.

She gasped, but he didn't stop kissing her. He added another finger and continued to pump into her while his tongue made love to her mouth.

Her breathing sped up and he moved his thumb to her clit, making small circles. Finding a rhythm, his thumb rubbed her bundle of nerves as his fingers moved deeper and faster into her.

When he felt her muscles tighten, he knew some dirty talk was what she needed to push her right over the edge. "Come for me, Kate. Come all over me. I want to feel your pussy squeeze the fuck out of my fingers."

Isaac pulled his head back so he could watch Kate's face as her orgasm claimed her, swamping her with pleasure. He loved seeing her in the throes of an orgasm and would have loved to give her another one, but he knew when patience was needed.

He gently pulled his fingers from her body, and while she watched, he put them in his mouth and sucked them clean. "Thank you, Kate."

Repeating her name was a way for him to make sure she knew he was in the moment and only thinking of her —that she was special to him. He leaned forward and placed a soft kiss on her lips, then flashed to his shop.

It wasn't quite like the way she had flashed out of his shower naked, but it was giving her exactly what she asked for. Isaac just hoped it wouldn't take Kate long to realize there was so much more he could give her.

AFTER ISAAC's last client of the day left, he flipped the lock on Ink Magic's front door. Turning around, Isaac noticed the calendar on the wall and smiled at the date—November fifteenth.

Exactly one year ago to the day he had agreed to stay in Blue Mountain, Colorado.

Instead of moving to the back of his shop, he stopped and took it all in—everything he had accomplished in the last year. The reception desk to his right was just below chest height. Underneath a sheet of glass, the desk's surface was painted in bright colors with one of his designs. The sitting area on his left held a couple of comfy couches, a coffee table, and side tables. Many of his drawings were framed and hung on the wall along with pictures his clients had sent him.

Ahead of him, the space was wide open. Four stations for tattoo artists were all set up but remained empty. The same as they had been for the entire year since Isaac had opened the shop.

When Jack had called him just over a year ago and invited him for a visit, Isaac hadn't imagined moving to Blue Mountain, Colorado. Salem, Oregon had been his home. But the only thing keeping him there were memories and grief. Even his mom had moved to a new city.

Listening to Meredith, Jack's girlfriend, now wife, while he gave her a memorial tattoo, and hearing her passion as she'd talked about the plans she had for her family's three buildings had sparked something within Isaac. Many factors influenced his decision to make Blue Mountain his home. Learning what Meredith had accomplished and still had planned had made Isaac want to be a part of that. He began to feel a bit like family when he met her cousins and everyone she and Jack had pulled into their circle. But the deciding factor was likely a certain auburn-haired beauty with a chip on her shoulder.

Isaac walked up to the first empty tattoo station and

waved his hand toward it, letting his magic flow out. He cleaned the area and left it sparkling before doing the same to the other three stations.

No matter how long he'd been a tattoo artist, looking at a group of tattoo stations always reminded him of his dad. He could picture his dad leaning over a large, bearded man while he tattooed his back. Isaac had sat on a stool just off to the side of his dad's shoulder, riveted to the tattoo machine's every movement. At fifteen, Isaac had already known that tattooing was his calling. He hadn't even thought about pursuing anything else.

Remembering his dad also made Isaac think of Austin. He had followed Isaac around like a little puppy, wanting to do everything his older brother did. Even with the five-year age gap, Isaac loved having his brother around. Although Isaac's friends thought they were too cool to have a younger sibling tag along, Isaac didn't. He always had time and patience for Austin. It didn't matter how many questions he asked or what he wanted, Isaac always gave in. Even the one time he shouldn't have.

Pushing the thought aside, he headed to the back of the shop and made quick work of cleaning up from his client. The booking had been last minute. When a friend from back home had called to see if Isaac could fit him in if he flashed to Blue Mountain, Isaac had said yes, knowing that Kate would have an excuse not to see him.

Earlier in the day, Isaac had hoped he could convince Kate to spend the evening with him. But after their little sexual challenge in her shop that afternoon, he knew she wouldn't agree to seeing him. But he would bet she was thinking of him. That was good enough for now.

Over the last year, he'd learned when and how much

to push Kate, and this was one of those times he needed to step back. At least for a while.

Isaac finished cleaning up and walked over to his desk, pulling out his stool. He picked up his coffee mug and peered inside, wondering if he needed to clean it. "It'll do," he mumbled to himself. He conjured some coffee, black and strong, the way he liked it, before taking a sip.

An update. Jack's message came into his mind as clear as if he had telecommunicated from only a few feet away. Isaac waited for the next part of the message. It had recently become routine for Jack to communicate with the council members and others associated with the Williams family, like Isaac, this way. Ever since Maverick had consumed evil magic and had begun attacking magics, both physically and through their minds, Jack wanted to make sure their group was kept up to date on current events. He would reach out to get everyone's attention and then wait a minute or two before passing on the message.

Most magics could only use telepathy over short distances, and even then, if they wanted to say more than a few words or a single sentence, they would need to stop and reestablish the connection. Not Jack. It was both handy and annoying that the man could interrupt at any given moment.

Isaac took another sip of his coffee and flicked at his tablet, waking it up, while he waited for Jack. The image on the screen was a dragon he'd drawn for his friend a short while ago. He flicked past it to the next sketch, one that was only partially complete. The image had come to Isaac in a dream a few nights before.

As soon as he'd woken up, he'd known the image, like

a vivid, breathing entity in his mind, could only be for Kate. One day, he'd have the pleasure of tattooing it on her. Only the when and the why were still a mystery. Most images that came to him in dreams were for tattoos —some magic, most not.

He hoped that this image was for something benign, like a birthday gift, but he got the feeling it wasn't. There wasn't anything specific that told him that, just a hunch that came from years of experience.

He set his coffee cup down and picked up his stylus just as another message from Jack entered his mind.

From now on, if you come into contact with Maverick or his minions, do not fight. I repeat. Do. Not. Fight. Flash to the fourth-floor boardroom above the bakery. Meredith and I will be alerted to your presence and will come to assist. Acknowledge.

Isaac sent his acknowledgment, and a small smile played at the corners of his lips. He wondered how Kate took the message. Although Jack sent it to all of them, what happened to Kate this afternoon may have prompted the new strategy. Isaac was sure he'd hear Kate's opinion about it soon enough. If she was talking to him, that was.

After their little tryst that afternoon, he was sure Kate would withdraw from him for a while. It wasn't what he wanted, but it would give him time to finish the design. But he would work on it now while the image was so clear in his mind. Only not in his empty shop because even though his apartment would be just as empty, it was more comfortable.

He tucked the stylus into his tablet and sent out his

magic to turn off the lights. Due to all the attacks on magics lately, he added a small protection spell to the front and back doors and flashed to his apartment.

Isaac kicked off his shoes at the entrance and walked through the open-concept design to the living room. He laid his tablet on the coffee table before flopping down on the couch.

He let his head fall back on the cushions and felt the tension from working hunched over leave his shoulders. The couch was one of his favorite things in the apartment. Maybe only second to the large glass shower stall. Thinking about the shower had him thinking about Kate again.

Isaac had been with Kate for almost the entire time he'd been in Blue Mountain, but he had only been in her house twice. Both times it was because he had stopped by unannounced.

Just like last week, she always flashed to his apartment. And she always had an excuse to explain why. He wasn't an idiot—he knew staying at his place meant she could leave any time she wanted. It also kept him out of her personal space.

The excuse she'd used last week was that there wasn't anything to eat in her house. "Nope, conjuring food would have been too difficult," he muttered to the empty room. The crazy thing was that they barely ate together anyway. He could count on one hand the number of dinners they had eaten together that weren't in The Magic Plate, surrounded by friends and family.

His stomach let out a loud growl, as if it heard him mention food. He sat forward and conjured a sandwich and a glass of water. As he ate, his eyes drifted to his tablet. Waking it up, he glanced at the partially finished sketch. The mosaic of swirls, flowers, and paisley would be feminine and intricate, and large enough to make a statement.

He would tattoo the design in black and gray with touches of turquoise woven throughout. The turquoise would have to be vibrant, a perfect complement to Kate's thick, red hair.

Isaac sat back against the cushions again, his sandwich finished. Closing his eyes, he pictured Kate's beautiful body. He could imagine inking the design so that it trailed up one of her long legs, starting on the top of her foot and winding around her ankle before ending at the top of her hip. Picturing his ink on Kate had him thinking back to what she'd looked like when he'd made her come that afternoon.

Using his magic, he removed his clothes and sent them to the laundry basket in his room. With his eyes still closed and his body relaxed, he palmed his cock and stroked himself slowly.

At first, he pictured Kate sitting on her workbench as he'd fucked her with his fingers. He tightened the grip on his dick and jerked faster as he remembered the feeling of Kate getting wetter.

Then his mind moved to the image of the way Kate looked in his shower, water streaming down around them as she rode him. He jacked himself off faster as to the memory of her digging her nails into him and yelling his name as she came all over his cock.

That visual sent him over the edge as he moaned and shot his load onto his stomach. When his breathing returned to normal, he conjured a towel and wiped himself off before sending it to the laundry basket to join his clothes.

A few minutes later, he pushed off the couch and made his way to his bedroom. He hoped to dream of Kate because he sure didn't know when he would see her again.

3

*K*ate closed the sliding glass door behind her as she stepped onto her back patio. The mountains weren't yet visible in the predawn darkness, but it didn't matter. She wasn't out there for the view. The crisp November air felt good against her skin. Cradling her coffee mug with both hands, she took a strong whiff of one of her favorite scents before taking her first sip.

Leaning back against the outside wall, she propped one foot behind her and stared out into the darkness. Her workshop sat about fifty yards away, and she could only just make out its shape because she was looking for it and knew it was there.

The building and everything it contained and represented was her pride and joy. She would never forget the day she'd signed on the dotted line and the two and a half acres with the three-bedroom Craftsman-style home became hers. Two weeks later when building supplies were delivered, and with some magic help from her family and friends, her workshop became a reality—The Stone Forge.

She huffed out a laugh at the memory of announcing the name. Damon had teased her about her lack of imagination. And her brother had been right; using their last name hadn't been very creative, but she'd shrugged it off.

Damon would never understand what it was like being a female in a male-dominated trade. How she was treated and used. At a hulking six foot three and with his commanding presence, he never had to prove himself the way she had. Never had to worry about men taking advantage of her just because they thought it was their right. But she had. Every. Day.

Putting her name on her business was a statement, and even though she hadn't justified it to her family, she hadn't apologized for it either. The Stone Forge was hers, and no man would ever be able to take it from her. Not that she associated with anyone who would try. At least not anymore.

Her circle of friends was small now and mostly female, although that was a change after being surrounded in her career by males for so long. A welcome change, though.

She took another sip of her coffee and the image of a certain non-female popped into her mind—Isaac. The man turned her on like no one else had and infuriated her at the same time. A part of her craved time with him, and another part of her wanted to stay far away. If anyone could make her vulnerable, it would be Isaac, but she would never put herself in that position again.

After the attack and the quick fuck in her workshop, she'd spent the rest of that day working. Yesterday, she'd ignored Isaac's two texts and holed up in her shop. It made her a chicken for not responding to his texts, but that didn't mean she was a coward for protecting her heart. She was losing a grip on what she had wanted with Isaac and she had to get it back.

Friends with benefits was all that she was willing to offer, and they had both agreed to it. Looking back, she knew that Isaac had wanted more right from the beginning, but she'd pushed, insisting on only sex or nothing. She'd been so sure she'd be able to keep it at that too. Even though she couldn't think of a way that Isaac could possibly use her like Ethan or the others had, it didn't mean Isaac wouldn't try to control her sooner or later. At some point, Isaac, like all men, would try to put her in a box, a place where he thought women belonged. He might want her to work less so she could spend more time with him, or look after their home, or give up her work to support him in his.

Like a coward, she'd hidden from the world yesterday and the night before. She wouldn't have talked to anyone if Jack hadn't called to let her know what the mirrors had revealed.

Now it was time. Instead of disappearing her coffee mug, she used her magic to clean it and went back into the house to put it away. After a quick stop in the bathroom, she tied her hair back and flashed to the inside of her shop.

The cinderblock walls didn't help keep the place warm when she wasn't using her forge, so she sent her magic out, clicking on the heaters and the lights. No matter how long she'd been a swordsmith, the anticipation of getting to create something from almost nothing sent anticipation running through her veins.

Today was no different, and yet it was. Her anticipation was cranked to a hundred. Jack said the mirrors revealed a sword, and he would send it to her today. That had been a surprise as she'd been expecting a piece of metal that she would make the needed lock from. Forging a lock from a sword didn't make much sense, but then, magic wasn't logical. If their ancestors thought storing the magic metal in the shape of a sword was the best solution, then who was she to argue?

Since she didn't know when Jack would bring the sword by—he had only said in the morning—or what she'd need to do, she wouldn't heat up her forge yet. She'd been so excited to see the sword that she'd wanted Jack to bring it by yesterday when he'd called, even though it had been late in the evening.

The sword had already killed one person, and Jack had wanted to check with other council leaders to make sure it would be safe for her to work with before he called her. Which explained the lateness of his call.

Kate went to her computer to check on new orders and ones she had in the pipeline. She'd been at it about twenty minutes when Jack sent her a telepathic message.

Incoming. I'll stop by tonight.

She looked up just as a bundled package appeared on her workbench.

Got it. She sent the message to Jack as she made her way to her workbench. The sword, at least she hoped that's what it was, lay wrapped in sheets of leather. "Okay, baby, let's see what you've got for me," she said to the sword, unable to contain her excitement.

She glanced at the clock on the wall, noting the time. Only six-thirty. Lots of time to decide how to tackle the sword. The only other item on her agenda for the day was lunch with her mom at twelve-thirty at The Magic Plate.

Using one of her blades, she cut through the rope holding the leather together. She laid the blade on her bench and unwrapped the sword with both hands. A gasp escaped her as she got her first look.

In the almost ten years she'd been working with metals, she'd seen a lot of swords, even designed some. But nothing had prepared her for this.

It was a broadsword, as Jack had said, and the blade was just over three feet in length with a width of about two-and-a-half-inches. Its grip added another four-and-a-half or five inches. It appeared to be a firework pattern, but more intricate than that. The pattern was a mosaic Damacus, and since it was magic, she had no idea what type of metal the blade was made from.

She shook her hands at the wrists, as if preparing to do something great, and laughed when she caught herself. But it *was* great. Touching an ancient magic sword wasn't something she did every day.

Because her magic allowed her to feel emotions in objects, mostly metal, she was hesitant to grasp the sword with both hands at once in case the emotions it emitted were overwhelming. She'd never been so excited yet so nervous to touch a sword before. Should she start with the blade or the handle?

Deciding on the blade as the handle might be ordinary steel, she gently touched it with the tips of all eight fingers at once.

A pulse of energy shot up her arms, jerking her shoulders, but her fingers stayed on the blade. The feelings in the blade settled down, sending a soothing current through her fingers.

She closed her eyes and relaxed her fingers to see if she could better sense what the blade was telling her.

"Kate! Kate, can you hear me? Kate, open your eyes!"

The sound of her mom's voice penetrated her mind as if it came from far away. She opened her eyes and pulled her hands off the blade, turning toward her mom. "What are you doing here? Not that I don't want to see you, Mom, but isn't six-thirty in the morning a bit early for you?"

Kate's mom grasped her upper arms and tugged her forward, closing her arms around her in a hug. "I didn't know if I could touch you," her mom whispered in her ear before pulling back.

"Mom, what are you talking about? What did you mean about not touching me?"

"Kate, it's not early. It's twelve-fifty-two. We were supposed to meet for lunch at twelve-thirty, remember?"

Kate whipped her head around to look at the clock on the wall. The digital display clicked over to twelve-fifty-three p.m. How was that even possible? She'd just touched the blade. Hadn't she? How had she lost over six hours?

She turned back to her mom and felt like the ocean had suddenly poured into her head because the roaring was so loud. She feared she wouldn't be able to hear anything else. Sending some magic through her body, she calmed her heartbeat, drowning out the sound of its frantic pounding. "I heard you yelling at me," she whispered while she tried to figure out what had happened.

"I flashed here and saw you touching the blade and didn't know what would happen if I touched you." Her mom's voice sounded shaky, and she took in a large breath. Maybe her heartbeat was as out of control as Kate's had been.

"All I wanted was to pull you away from it," her mom continued, sounding a bit steadier. "But I didn't know what would happen. It was like you were in a trance."

"I thought I'd only touched it for a few minutes."

Her mom frowned, a look Kate was far too familiar with. "But you also thought it was still six-thirty in the morning."

Kate didn't respond as it wasn't a question.

Her mom pulled her phone from her pocket and put it to her ear.

"Wait, who are you calling?"

"Damon, I need you to come to Kate's forge," her mom said into the phone, speaking right over her.

"Fuck," she whispered, hoping her mom didn't hear. "You didn't have to call Damon, you know," she said in a louder voice. "I don't need my brother—or any man—to protect me." Since she knew who her brother was spending the day with, it was likely that he wouldn't show up alone.

ISAAC OPENED the photo app on his tablet as he sat on a stool next to Damon, who was perched on the edge of the tattoo chair.

Damon had booked the appointment almost two months ago—right after he and Morgana came back from Mexico. Working with a friend and having a challenging design was just what Isaac needed. More thankful than he'd cared to admit that he had something to keep his mind off Kate after she continued to ignore him, he looked at Damon. "Thanks for sending the pictures of Morgana's tattoo. I'm still a bit in awe every time I think about how some of the pieces changed."

"It shocked us too."

"My dad told me stories about tattoos breaking spells, so that didn't surprise me. But parts changing into something else… That was definitely a first for me." Isaac gave Damon a smirk. "Out of all the pieces of Morgana's tattoo you could copy, you want the serpent, huh? Cunning and manipulative. Your ability of persuasion not enough?"

Damon cracked a smile. "According to Morgana, it is. But to be honest…" His expression sobered. "If Morgana hadn't resisted my persuasion, I would have prevented her from finding Sam. I can't imagine…" He rubbed his right cheek. He'd come back from Mexico with a raised scar covering that cheek, and it ended just below his eye. "So I don't regret this, and since no amount of magic will heal it, I'll always have it as a reminder of what we went through. But I'd like one that's a little more positive. And one of my own choosing," he said, looking Isaac in the eyes. "I want it on my forearm where I'll see it all the time."

"Understood." Isaac flicked through the pictures from Damon until he found the close-up of Morgana's serpent. After he studied it for a few minutes, he switched to his drawing program and began to sketch. The original sunflower he'd tattooed on Morgana had been small, only about an inch in length, and the serpent it had transformed into wasn't much bigger.

Isaac used the full length of his tablet for the design, knowing he could print the stencil in any size Damon wanted. He didn't talk as he drew freehand, adding detail as he went.

When he was finished, he turned the tablet around and watched Damon's face to gauge his feelings on the piece.

"Wow, man, you're talented. Amazing. I know that's exactly what I asked for..." Damon hesitated, as if he wanted to say something else.

"But..." Isaac prompted.

"I'm not sure." Damon took the tablet and studied it closely for a few moments.

Isaac knew why Damon hesitated because he'd felt the same thing. Something was missing from the sketch. Not from the serpent, but from the design as a whole. He took the tablet when Damon passed it back. "You open to adding something to the design?"

"Sure, but I can't see the other transformed pieces working."

"Agreed. But an idea just came to me and I think you'll like it."

"Show me."

Isaac saved his current sketch as version one and went back to drawing. He'd drawn the serpent in an S-type shape with the bottom curling around itself. In his mind, he saw a large sunflower coming out of the loop formed by the curled tail, with the stems and leaves of the smaller sunflowers surrounding the rest of the serpent. With the image so clear in his mind, he was able to draw quickly, and then he moved to the next addition. On the bottom of the serpent's tail, he added a butterfly that looked like it was about to take flight.

"I picture all of it in black and gray, except for the butterfly," he said as he handed the tablet over to Damon.

Damon took in the sketch but didn't say anything. Isaac hadn't expected him to as sometimes it took a while to absorb the impact of the full design. Sometimes his designs even surprised him.

"I'd like a copy of this to frame," Damon said when he handed the tablet back. "It's perfect."

"Great. Now let's talk about the colors for the butterfly and get it transferred to a stencil."

Damon decided on vibrant blues, and since Isaac had blocked out the rest of the day for the appointment, he figured they would get it finished in one sitting.

It didn't take long to get the stencil the right size and the design transferred to Damon's skin.

"Did you ever hear the story about why Morgana got the serpent?" Damon asked after Isaac had been tattooing for a few minutes.

Isaac kept his focus on his work as he answered. "No. But I heard all about the fire and gravity."

"Yeah, that was something I never want to go through again." Damon made a huffing noise. "The serpent was the second flower to change, the first being the butterfly when the spell broke. Anyway… we had gone to the apartment where she'd been held, and I was worried she was going to do something reckless. Since the spell on her had only just broken and her magic hadn't returned yet, I figured I could use a little magic persuasion to make sure she stayed safe."

Isaac glanced up at Damon with a grin. "And how did that work out for you?"

Damon chuckled. "At first, I thought it had. I should

have known better. Morgana has always been stubborn, even as a little girl."

"I know all about stubborn women," Isaac muttered as he worked.

"Talking about my sister by any chance? She's always..." Damon stopped talking when his phone rang, and he shifted onto his hip so he could pull it out of his pocket. "It's my mom. Just a second..." He answered the call and then paused. "What?"

Damon's harsh tone was a surprise. The man revered his mother and never treated her with anything but respect.

Pushing to his feet, Damon shoved his phone back into his pocket. "The sword did something to Kate. She's at her forge."

Isaac didn't need to hear anything else. He flashed.

4

Kate didn't even have time to brace herself before Damon and Isaac appeared in her workshop.

"What happened?" Isaac demanded as he stalked toward her.

Before he could pull her into his arms like she suspected he wanted to, she took a step back and held up her hands. "I'm fine. I just lost track of time and missed my lunch date with Mom. She overreacted when I didn't show up."

"Katherine Jennifer Stone!" Kate flinched at her mother's use of her full name. "I do not panic or overreact. Ever!"

"Kate," Damon said as he took a step toward her, his eyes scanning her from head to toe as if checking for injuries. "Mom's right, she's not one to overreact. Tell us what happened."

Maybe if she hurried through her explanation, everyone would leave her alone and she could get back to the sword. The fact that she'd touched the blade for six hours was still a little hard to fathom, but there had to be a reason. The unawareness of time passing had to mean something, and she wanted to know what that was.

Straightening her shoulders, she put on an air of bravado she'd perfected over the years while working in a man's world. When she raised her voice over the others, she projected confidence, even if she didn't feel it. "When Jack sent the sword, I unwrapped it. It's a stunning piece of art and craftsmanship. I just got caught up in studying it and lost track of time."

"You were more than *caught up*," her mom said, emphasizing Kate's phrasing. "When I arrived—"

"What's going on?" Jack boomed from where he'd landed near the door of her shop.

Kate flicked her eyes over to Jack as he walked up to Damon's side.

"Good thing you're here, Jack," her mom said, and Kate held in a groan of frustration.

"Damon reached out," Jack said and nodded at Damon.

Great. One more person, and another man at that, to see that she'd lost control of the situation with the sword. She called on her magic and pushed a cooling breeze through her chest, neck, and face to combat the heat she felt rising in her skin. The last thing she needed was for her embarrassment to be obvious. It was bad enough that everyone was here. She wanted to know why she hadn't had control and the only way to figure that out was to get back to the sword. To do that, she needed everyone to leave.

Facing Jack, she once more projected confidence. "I lost track of time. That's all. Everyone is making a big deal out of nothing. I. Am. Fine." All that mattered was for everyone to take her seriously and trust her so they would skedaddle.

Her mom turned to Jack as if Kate hadn't even spoken. "Kate was supposed to meet me for lunch at twelve-thirty at The Magic Plate. After fifteen minutes, she still hadn't arrived so I called her in case she'd gotten caught up with work. When she didn't answer, I flashed over here and found her in a trance. Her fingers were on the sword's blade, and it took me calling her several times before she even acknowledged me. Then she was surprised to see me because she thought it was still six-thirty in the morning." Her gaze flicked to Kate before focusing back on Jack. "That's not just losing track of time."

"I had the sword checked by other council leaders, and they truly believed that the blade was safe to touch as long as the person touching it didn't have evil intent. I wouldn't have given it to Kate if I thought it would cause her harm," Jack said. "I'm truly sorry, Fiona."

Her mom dismissively waved her hand at Jack. "I know you wouldn't have. It's just that while I was waiting for Kate, I…" Her mom's eyes flicked to her again before looking back at Jack, her gaze encompassing Damon and Isaac as well. "I had a vision of Kate."

"What?" Kate shrieked. "Mom, why didn't you tell me?" A vision. Fucking fantastic. That was all she needed for this little group of testosterone-laden alphas to get even more protective.

"It was only just before I went to meet you for lunch. I was going to tell you then."

"Fiona," Isaac said, getting her mom's attention. "What

happened in the vision?" Isaac came over to Kate but didn't touch her as he waited for her mom to continue.

Kate felt just like she had the other day. She wanted to lean into Isaac and let him support her, but if she did, she'd show him her vulnerable side, and then he could walk all over her. She took a step away from him.

"It wasn't much, just a flash of an image. But I saw Kate lying on the floor in a white room. She looked like she was unconscious."

Her mom looked over at her, and Kate felt swamped with shame. All she wanted was to be seen as strong and capable so no one would ever use her again, but in standing up for herself, she had dismissed her mom's concerns. For Kate's entire life, her mom had seen visions, and as far as she knew, they had all come true.

Walking up to her mom, Kate pulled her into a hug. "I'm sorry for scaring you, Mom," she whispered against her mom's hair. Her mom meant the world to her and was one of the only people who she didn't have to prove herself with. Hurting her mom was inexcusable.

Kate pulled back, and her mom kissed her cheek. "I know, honey." And just like that, her mom forgave her. Not many people were like that.

"Jack," her mom said. "You didn't get a vision at all?"

"Of Kate?" Jack shook his head. "No."

That didn't sound reassuring. It meant that Jack did have a vision, and lately anytime someone had a vision, it let them know there was bad news in their future. Too bad her mom and Jack couldn't have had visions of a shoe sale.

Kate half-turned her body and pointed at her bench where the sword still lay. She needed to get back to work and make sure that no one made a decision for her. "Since I'm okay, I'm going to go back to—"

Her brother spoke right over her, cutting her off as if she hadn't said anything. "Isaac, can you give Kate a tattoo that will protect her when she's working on the sword?"

She directed a smile her brother's way. At least he wasn't trying to stop her from working on the sword. Well... not exactly. But now her fate rested in Isaac's hands.

KATE HADN'T MOVED BACK near Isaac after she'd gone to hug her mom, so he stepped up beside her. When she looked into his eyes, a sense of foreboding came over him. The same one that he'd had when he knew the tattoo in his dream was going to be for something big. Only this time, the feeling was stronger.

For the first time since becoming intimate with Kate, he hesitated for a fraction of a second as he reached for her. Then, pushing away any doubts, he held Kate's upper arms, ready to accept whatever feelings and impressions his magic pushed to him.

The connection that came at him was immediate and more powerful than he'd ever felt with anyone. Almost like something in her was reaching for him. But it wasn't the same type of feeling he got when sensing whether or not to do a memorial tattoo. His magic wasn't telling him yes or no, only that the feeling was powerful—which didn't give him an answer.

Closing his eyes, he pushed more of his magic into his

hands and waited. He was just about to let go and agree to ink Kate when he felt a pushback on his hands. It wasn't like when Isabella had asked him about a memorial tattoo for her brother and his magic had been repelled by the idea. This was subtle.

Trying to empty his mind of all thoughts, he focused on the feelings swirling inside him. He knew he cared deeply for Kate, and perhaps that was interfering with his ability to detect the truth. Once more, he pushed all other thoughts aside and concentrated on sensing what had pushed back.

Isaac was at a loss. When his brother had asked him for a memorial tattoo, his magic hadn't pushed back as strongly as it had with Isabella, but the feeling was still there. Austin had been relentless in his pleading, and eventually, Isaac had given in. The one time he should have held his ground.

Maybe this was the second time. Isaac refused to risk it.

He dropped his hands and stepped back from Kate before meeting her gaze. "I'm sorry, Kate, I can't do it." Isaac counted down in his head but didn't break eye contact with her, knowing the full force of Kate's ire was about to be unleashed upon him. Three. Two. One.

"Can't?" Kate asked, barely below a shout. Her hands landed on her hips as she thrust her upper body toward him. "Or won't?"

"It doesn't matter," he said quietly. "The outcome is the same. I won't ink you so you can touch the sword, Kate. It's not safe."

Kate took a step toward him, getting in his way, but he couldn't back down. "Why, Isaac? If it's not safe, that's my decision to decide whether or not it's worth the risk!"

All he wanted to do was pull her into his arms and tell her how much he cared for her and that he wouldn't put her life at risk. Even if it meant she couldn't work on a sword that could save thousands. She meant more to him than all the other magics on the planet. But he didn't say any of that because she wouldn't want to hear it. Keeping his voice calm, he said the only thing she might listen to. "No, Kate. It's my choice and I won't risk it."

"Fuck you, Isaac!" she hissed. "I knew trusting you would come back to bite me in the ass one of these days! Maybe if I hadn't slept with you, you'd treat me like everyone else."

Kate's hatred cut deep into his soul, but he wouldn't change his mind. He'd made that mistake once before, and it cost him more than he ever could have imagined.

"I can't believe you're—"

"Kate! That's enough!" Fiona said, cutting off Kate's newest rant. "Isaac has to trust his gift, just like we all have to trust our own. Now..."

Isaac finally looked away from Kate. Her anger felt like a tangible force aimed directly at him. Turning away from her felt like he had severed a bond he would never get back, but he'd made the right choice. Maybe Fiona could get Kate to see his side.

"Jack," Fiona continued. "What do you want to do?"

"I don't know yet." Jack held out his hand, and the sword—leather cloth and all— lifted from Kate's work-bench and soared through the air like it was on a bungee cord attached to Jack. The wrapped bundle hit Jack's hand, his fingers closing around it. "I'll take it for now and put a cloaking spell on it. I'll have Meredith give me a hand, and hopefully the magic from both of us will make the spell strong enough to hide it from Maverick and his minions."

"No! Jack, you can't take it," Kate pleaded. "I need it to make the lock for the box. You said yourself locking the box is the only way to hold the evil that's inside Maverick. If we don't do it soon, he'll infect more magics."

"Believe me, Kate. I know what's at stake. All the magics under my council's purview *are* my top concern," Jack said, his gaze locked on Kate. "And that includes you. I don't want to put anyone at risk, especially someone I consider family." Jack turned to Fiona. "I'm sorry, Fiona. I should have protected Kate. I'm sure Maverick knows by now that we have the sword and will be working to get it back. The first place he'll probably look is here. I'll assign some people to watch Kate. It doesn't—"

"No!" Kate yelled, interrupting Jack. "I won't let you have people guard me like some helpless damsel in a castle!"

"Kate, please be reasonable," Damon said.

Isaac bit back a smile before it could fully form. The look on Damon's face told Isaac that the big man realized too late what he had said. Three, two, one...

"Be reasonable?" Kate's anger hissed out through clenched teeth. "You think I'm not being reasonable, Damon?" Kate's voice grew louder with each word. "There are people being controlled and dying, Damon! I can forge the lock that could stop all that!"

"Kate, that's not—" Damon tried to backpedal, but it was too late; he'd already kicked the hornet's nest.

"Oh, I get exactly what you meant, big brother!"

"Stop!" Jack projected into the group, and even Isaac felt the push of magic that accompanied it. "If I want to post sentries, I will. It's not your decision to make, Kate." Jack turned to Isaac and nodded. "Thank you for trying."

Then Jack left, sword and all.

"Isaac, we'll have to finish another time. I have a sudden compulsion to check on Morgana. I'm out of here," Damon said, and then he too flashed away.

Fiona walked up to her daughter. "Kate, honey. After the vision and then seeing you in a trance, I had to call in help."

Kate's shoulders dropped like a pin had popped her anger balloon. "It's okay, Mom. I get it." She gave her mom a kiss on the cheek before Fiona flashed away.

It was only him and Kate left now. Even though he cared about Kate, he wasn't naïve enough to think she'd forgive him as easily.

She turned to him, and he saw the defeat in her eyes. That cut him deeper than her anger. Kate's passion and determination were just two of her many traits that he admired. To think that he was responsible for distinguishing her light was a hard pill to swallow.

"Why, Isaac? Why won't you let me decide if I'm willing to take the risk? It should be my choice," she said softly, reinforcing the fact that he'd destroyed the fight in her.

"It's not your choice, Kate. It's my magic that gets pushed into the design, which makes it my responsibility."

"Because you don't trust me," she said quietly before flashing away.

Isaac fell forward, putting his hands on his knees as he tried to catch his breath. Kate's comment had ripped the breath from his lungs, making it difficult to breathe. She wasn't the first person to say those words to him. Austin had said the same thing.

Isaac had given in and inked his brother against his better judgment, and it had cost him everything. He wouldn't do it again. Kate might hate him, but at least she'd be alive to bitch about it.

5

"Thank you," Kate said to the server as the woman placed her meal on the table.

"This looks good," she said to Isabella. "And thanks again for coming out with me. A little retail therapy and a meal out was just what I needed today."

"Thanks for asking me… It's been a tough week."

"I'll say." Kate kept her voice low. They'd taken a table at the back of the restaurant. The place wasn't packed since it was early for the dinner crowd, yet they were still careful. When they'd been shopping, they had kept their talk to clothes in case they were overheard. The last thing they needed was someone recording them talking about magic.

"You've had quite the week. Jack gave everyone the bare details about what happened with the sword… I haven't had a chance to say anything before now, but… I'm sorry about your brother." She wasn't quite sure what to say. Isabella's brother had been responsible for Kate being attacked and he had hurt many of her friends, yet he'd still been Isabella's brother. Being close to her own brother, Kate couldn't imagine him ever turning on her. Even when Damon drove her crazy with his persuasive gift and overprotective ways, she loved him. She had no idea what Isabella must be feeling.

Isabella gave her a small smile. "Thanks."

They dug into their meals, and neither of them spoke for a few minutes until Kate felt compelled to break the silence. "I… I'm not sure what to say…"

Isabella met Kate's gaze.

"I don't know what you're going through… but I'm here if you want to talk." Kate leaned forward and lowered her voice to a whisper. "Since it's only been just over a week since everything happened, I'm guessing you haven't even processed it all yet." She made her words a statement instead of a question so Isabella could choose how she answered.

"I think you're right, but Reece has been a big help." Another small smile curled Isabella's lips, but this time, a sense of love radiated from her instead of sadness.

Even though Kate thought of Reece as a brother, she felt a stirring of jealousy for what Isabella had. Not that Kate wanted it for herself, because she'd learned her lesson. But maybe she was envious. She'd once thought she could have what Isabella had. Now she knew better and couldn't go back to her naïve way of thinking. Even though Kate wouldn't take any of her old boyfriends back for anything, what she'd been through had opened her eyes. Sure, maybe Reece was different, as were the men her friends had hooked up with, but most men weren't. Especially with women like Kate—women who lived in a man's world and who threatened their masculinity.

A few minutes later, Kate felt Isabella's eyes on her and looked up. "Your meal okay?"

"It's good. Thanks for inviting me today... It's been a good break."

"I'm glad."

"Now spill it. I know why I needed a break, but what prompted this shopping trip for you?" Isabella asked, surprising Kate.

She took a sip of water to give herself time to compose her thoughts. Their friendship was new, but she liked Isabella, and they were both strong, independent women. Maybe getting another woman's opinion would be a good thing.

Kate laid down her fork. "I thought I'd be working with the sword, or probably even finished creating the lock by now. Instead, I'm frustrated and angry because it's been eight days since Jack took the sword away. He said he was going to figure out how to make it safe for me to work with it. But in the meantime, I've been stuck with a shadow at my workshop."

"A shadow?"

"Yes. A shadow in the form of an FBI agent appointed by Jack because everyone thinks I can't take care of myself. Now I've got someone watching me work all day. It's super annoying."

"I don't think that's why Jack posted a guard."

Kate snorted and then looked around to see if she'd caught anyone's attention with the sudden loud noise. When she didn't see anyone looking at them, she turned back to Isabella. "Really? Do you have someone watching you all day?"

Isabella flashed a grin. "Actually, I do. Reece has barely

left my side." Her smile fell. "I understand why Reece is so worried, considering what happened to us. Then there was my brother's internment—"

"Oh shit." Kate reached across the table and gave Isabella's hand a squeeze before pulling back. "I'm so sorry I didn't say anything; I was too caught up in my own shit. It was just a few days ago, right?"

Isabella nodded. "Only three, but I'm doing okay. It was—oh my god! Now it's my turn to forget to say something." Isabella pulled her sleeve up a few inches and shoved her wrist at Kate. "Look what Isaac gave me. It's only four days old, but Reece healed it."

"Let me get a better look," Kate said as she jumped up from her chair and went around to Isabella. Standing behind the chair, she looked over her friend's shoulder so she could see the tattoo the way Isabella saw it. "A compass—I love it. It seems perfect for you as you were a traveler and now you're settling down here. You've found your way."

"Thanks. And you're right, I have."

Kate went back to her chair. "Is it the same design that Meredith, Jo, and Rowena have?"

"Yes, but it's not a memorial tattoo like theirs. Isaac said he couldn't do one for me."

"He seems to be saying no a lot lately," Kate muttered.

"What do you mean? He wouldn't do a memorial tattoo for you?"

"Not a memorial one, but one to keep me safe while I work on the sword. He wouldn't do it… or he can't do it. I don't remember which. Anyway… he doesn't trust me." Kate heard the bitterness in her own voice.

Isabella leaned over the table, closing the space

between them. "You know the sword killed my brother, right?" she asked quietly.

"What? No. No one told me that. I only knew that he died, and that the sword killed someone, but not who." Kate couldn't seem to get much right lately. "I'm sorry, Isabella."

Sitting back, Isabella waved her hand in front of her face. Kate wasn't sure if Isabella had meant it as a sign of dismissal or if she was magically drying her tears. "It's okay. But what I meant is that the sword is dangerous. You're lucky people care about you so much that they want to protect you."

Kate's shoulders tensed at Isabella's comments, but she refused to take her anger out on her friend. She was reserving all her anger for the one who actually deserved it. "I can protect myself."

"Really? Like you protected yourself against my brother in your shop? Or what about the trance I heard you went into?"

Not sure whether she should get her back up at Isabella's words or be ashamed at her own weakness for having not been able to defend herself, Kate kept quiet.

"Kate, I'm not trying to be mean. I just don't think you know what we're dealing with. No one can defend themselves against Maverick. He almost killed me and Reece, and he's turning more and more magics against their own kind every day. He's too powerful, and he's passing that power on to others to do his bidding. Eddie had strength I couldn't even imagine."

A sense of shame washed over Kate. Something she was becoming all too familiar with lately. She had felt shame for being weak. Then for taking her frustration out on her mom. Now she felt it for being self-centered and making everything about her. Not once had she considered the dangers other magics were going through.

"I'm sorry, Isabella. I've been too caught up in my own shit."

"It's okay. We all get like that," she said with a smirk. "When all this mess is over and we get back to big family dinners, you can ask Reece all about what my own selfishness almost did. Believe me, I get it."

"Thanks." Kate wished the understanding words could wash away her shame, but she feared it was too ingrained to be cleansed away so easily. Getting rid of her shame would mean dissolving the anger she felt from her past, something she didn't think she would ever let go of.

Pushing the thoughts aside, she decided to change the subject. "So, tell me… how did you get your totally in love and protective boyfriend to let you come out with me today?"

Isabella's eyes crinkled at the corners as she smiled. "It wasn't an easy feat, but I managed to turn his love of spells against him."

If Kate could only be so lucky with Isaac. "Do tell," she teased.

"In the last couple of days, Reece started going through all the spellbooks I think he had already been through dozens of times. After everything we went through, he's determined to find a spell for every situation we could possibly get ourselves into. Just in case, he said. So, as a game, I started throwing out scenarios to see if he had a spell to go with it."

Kate knew a devious plot when she heard one and liked the thought of being able to pull one over on a domineering male. Especially if it used something he loved. "Like what? How to ward off a bear attack?"

"Oh, that's a good one. I'll have to ask Reece about that next time. So no, I didn't use that one, but you get the idea. I knew he had a locator spell because he's used it to find me. But I feigned innocence and asked about other spells I was sure he had, like soundproofing a room, keeping out pests, and creating a message to pop up at a specific time."

"Did he have a spell for all those things?"

"Yep." A devious look crossed Isabella's face. "Then I went in for the kill."

"Oh my god. What did you ask?"

"I asked if he had a spell that someone could use to protect themselves in a dangerous situation. One that would do more than just what using their own magic would do. Like to repel harm if they were out on their own."

Kate laughed. "And Reece hadn't caught on yet?"

"Oh, he had, but by then it was too late."

"I'm guessing he had one?"

"He did, and he knew I wouldn't let him get away with not giving it to me." Isabella curled her fingers and blew on her nails before pretending to buff them on her shirt, as if to say she was hot stuff. "That's why I'm here without my shadow. I'll get Reece to give it to you. I'd do it, but I can't remember all of it."

"It can wait. And when I get it, I'll suggest he give it to Jack so it can be passed on to anyone who might need it." Kate wondered if that was all Isaac wanted—to make sure she was safe, not to control her. Second-guessing herself was not a good feeling.

Isabella snapped her fingers. "Good idea. Like the one that stopped Maverick from getting inside our heads."

"Enough about safety," Kate said, wanting to drop the topic. "How about some dessert? I heard this place has the best chocolate fudge cake and that the pieces are massive. Want to share a piece?"

"Share? You sure it'll be big enough for the two of us?" Isabella teased.

"Hmm… maybe." Kate laughed and looked around to see if their server was nearby when a shout came from the front of the restaurant. A man ran past the hostess station, and mid-stride, he turned sideways, shooting a bolt of magic toward the entrance as someone burst through the door.

"Get down!" Kate whisper-yelled as she lunged at Isabella and grabbed hold of her arm, pulling them both to the floor and rolling under the table.

"I need a short stretch break," Isaac said as he wiped a paper towel over the new ink on Damon's arm before putting down his tattoo machine.

"Sounds good," Damon said, getting up. "I'll use the restroom."

Isaac stood and rotated his neck from side to side. He'd been hunched over for a couple of hours already. During their last session, he hadn't finished the outline before they'd rushed to Kate's, which meant that he had almost started from the beginning again.

Thinking of Kate made him want to check his phone to see if she'd texted, but he knew she hadn't. After she'd flashed away last week, believing he didn't trust her, his texts and calls had gone unanswered.

For three full days, he'd let her sulk until he had finally had enough and took matters into his own hands. He'd flashed directly onto her front doorstep. It took fifteen minutes of him standing in the cold and talking to her through the door before she had finally opened it.

No matter how he looked at it, he couldn't call her eventual greeting welcoming, but at least she let him into her house. As soon as she shut the door behind him, he'd tried to get her to sit down and talk. But Kate's emotional walls were higher than he'd ever seen them.

Getting right into his space, her lips had been only a hair's breadth from his when she told him she needed a good fuck. That was all she'd wanted from him. Or at least all she was willing to admit that she wanted. He hated the friends-with-benefits box she had put them into, but he wasn't going to turn down any time he got to spend with her, horizontal or not.

In his mind, it was more than sex when they were together—he was making love to her. Maybe it was that way for her too, but that was likely another thing she wasn't willing to admit.

He had willingly given her what she wanted, but once more, it had been on his terms. Flipping their positions so he was the one with his back to the room, he had backed her up until she was sandwiched between the wall and his body. Ridding her of her clothes only took a second using his magic, and then he had fingered her to two orgasms. She'd begged for Isaac to fuck her, but he wasn't going to give her everything she wanted, at least not yet.

Now she was talking to him, although he had initiated all the phone calls, and their conversations over the last few days had all revolved around sex. Tonight, he had planned to stop by her house and bring dinner, hoping they could eat and talk. Do something more than just fuck. His internal whining that all his girlfriend wanted was sex would likely be enough to have his man-card revoked if any of his male friends heard him. But one of the biggest problems was that Kate didn't see herself as his girlfriend, even though Isaac did.

Unfortunately, his plan to have dinner wasn't going to work. Kate had texted him earlier to say she was going shopping and out for dinner with Isabella. The text had surprised him—it was the first since she had started talking to him again. A simple text wasn't much, but since Kate had let him know what she was doing instead of keeping him hanging, he considered it a win.

"Ready to get back to it?" Damon asked, interrupting Isaac's thoughts.

"Sure."

They both got back into position, and Isaac started back up. He was really pleased with Damon's tattoo and figured they'd have it finished in another couple of hours.

"I fucking love it," Damon said a few minutes later. "Good call on adding to the design. Glad you didn't leave it up to me."

"No problem."

"How did you come up with Morgana's design?"

"Sometimes ideas pop into my head. Or like with Morgana's, I see them in a dream."

"You definitely outdid yourself with that one. I know you put it on both sides of her body to help break the spell cast on her, but man... it's beautiful, the way it frames her."

"Thanks. I've done a lot of vines and flowers, but I've never done anything exactly like that design before."

They chatted for a few minutes about some of the tattoo designs that Isaac considered most memorable. Then they lapsed back into a comfortable silence while Isaac worked.

"I've never known you to be an overly chatty guy," Damon said about an hour later. "But you seem quieter than usual. Any chance your mood has something to do with you refusing to tattoo Kate last week?

"You could say that."

"Morgana and I went to my mom's for dinner the other night, and Kate was there. She was still pretty grumpy, although sometimes that's just par for the course with my sister."

Isaac didn't look up as he continued to work. "Yeah, grumpy is a good description for Kate. Stubborn works too. I don't know why she won't just accept that I can't give her the tattoo."

"Really? You're surprised?" Damon laughed. "I thought you knew my sister."

Isaac smirked. "Right, okay, she's a bit tenacious when she wants something. And stubborn. I've never met a more stubborn woman."

"She's driven, that's for sure. But she's also been hurt in the past, making it hard for her to trust people."

Stilling his machine, Isaac looked up and met Damon's gaze. "Who hurt her?"

"Not my story to tell. You'll have to ask her. But I am curious about you."

"About?"

"Why won't you give Kate the tattoo?"

"I listen to my magic."

"And it told you not to tattoo Kate?"

"Sort of." Since Isaac's magic worked on feelings and sensations, it wasn't always easy to explain. Sometimes he got a definite response, like he'd had with Isabella the other day. Other times, he got an inkling of what it was trying to tell him, and he hoped Damon would under-stand his explanation. "It's not always black and white, so I have to guess what my magic is trying to tell me. With Kate, it felt like a warning not to ink her."

"In a way, I get that. There have been a couple of times when I've gotten some pushback on my persuasion."

When Damon paused, Isaac prepared to start up again, but then he continued speaking.

"So, let's say you got a warning and you ignored it. What's the worst that could happen?"

"Death."

"Fuck. Really? One of your tattoos could kill someone?"

The familiar weight of guilt settled on Isaac. And like always, he wished his magic specialty was more precise. "I'm not sure. I refused to give someone a tattoo once, but they wouldn't stop bugging me, so I gave in. The tattoo caused them to sink into a deep depression until they eventually committed suicide."

"Fuck, man. I'm sorry."

Isaac nodded and got back to work.

"Did you warn the person about what you sensed?" Damon asked a few minutes later.

"Yes, but like I said, they wouldn't drop it."

"So, they made the choice to go ahead, even knowing the risk?"

"They made the choice, but I'll never know whether they truly understood the risk. Not even I knew. Now I don't give a person the choice. If I think it's dangerous, I won't do it."

They dropped back into silence and worked for about a half hour before they took another break. An hour after that, Isaac only needed to add a few more finishing touches.

"We're being sexist, you know," Damon said out of the blue.

Isaac stopped working and looked up. "What? You've lost me."

"Sorry, I was thinking about Morgana and Kate. We call them stubborn, but that's being sexist."

"How so?"

"If a man is stubborn, he's considered assertive and applauded for going after what he wants. He's thought to know his own mind, and that's a good thing."

"Hmm." Isaac considered that for a moment and realized Damon was right; it wasn't the first time he'd heard something like that. Isaac just hadn't equated it to Kate. Like all the men Isaac had become friends with since moving to Blue Mountain, they appreciated that the women they knew and loved were strong and independent. "I just wish Kate wouldn't put herself in danger."

Damon barked a laugh. "Oh? Like when Morgana went down to Mexico on her own to face off with a cartel? Or when Meredith marched right into the lion's den to find her mother? What about when Jo tricked that asshole Snake to save Simon? How about when Rowena went out on her own and—"

"Okay, okay. I got it," Isaac said, interrupting Damon. "I've just never felt like this about anyone..." Isaac let the sentence hang and focused on his work for a moment. Damon was his friend, but Isaac wasn't sure how much to say. After all, Kate was his sister. Isaac didn't have a sister and had never needed to worry about that whole bro-code shit about not going out with a friend's sister. Not like it seemed that Damon cared about that. Isaac just wondered about how much to share.

"I'll never want the dirty details, but I know you care about my sister," Damon said as if reading Isaac's mind. "She would be lucky to have you—you're a good guy. And as for you, you'd be damn lucky to have Kate's love. I happen to think my sister is amazing."

Isaac felt the corners of his lip curl up as he looked at Damon. "Amazing and assertive? Strong and independent? Not willing to listen to reason?"

"Yeah, all that too."

Isaac was just asking Damon if he wanted him to heal the tattoo for him, a perk of them being magic, when Jack reached out.

Everyone to the boardroom. Now.

KATE ROLLED off Isabella and moved into a crouching position. "Stay hidden," she whispered, shuffling over to give Isabella more room.

"What happened?" Isabella asked, whispering too.

"A guy just ran in and aimed a bolt of magic at someone following him."

"In public? What the—" Isabella cut herself off as her eyes widened in shock. Kate understood how she felt.

The restaurant had become a cacophony of sounds—crying, shouting, and banging that sounded like furniture was being overturned.

"All magics show yourself!" a voice boomed with the

volume of a megaphone. Kate guessed the man had used magic to project his voice.

"Holy shit!" Kate whispered. "They're outing magics. Maverick has to be behind this. Maybe he's trying to flush out magics to get them to follow him."

"Or kill them."

"Fuck. I didn't even think of that."

"I've got to look," Kate said quietly and began to scoot out from under the table.

Isabella tugged on her arm and pulled Kate toward her to whisper in her ear. "Wait. Let's just flash out of here."

"We can't. Look." Flicking her chin toward the next table, Kate directed Isabella's gaze. Other patrons had taken similar cover under tables, leaving anything Kate and Isabella did visible. "Non-magics will see us."

"Magics have already been exposed. Would we really make it any worse?"

Turning her head, she gave Isabella a look she hoped said, *Are you crazy?* "Right now, any non-magics are probably totally confused and have rationalized that the shot of magic was a large muzzle flash. If we suddenly vanished into thin air, it will be the first thing people will tell the police and news crews when they arrive. Plus, we don't know if the restaurant has cameras that could catch us flashing."

"Right. I wasn't thinking. There hasn't been another call for magics again, and it's gotten kind of quiet. Maybe they've left. Take a look, but be careful."

Kate nodded. Already facing the front of the room, she scooted backward so she could come up on the back side of the table. It wouldn't be much cover, but she wanted the table between her and the guys in the front, hoping they wouldn't see her.

Sending some magic to her legs for a bit of extra strength and support, she balanced on half-bent knees without needing to hold onto anything. Using visible magic in public wasn't something she ever thought she'd need to do, but she wanted her hands free in case she needed to get off a blast of power.

She shoved up, her eyes just above the edge of the table. "Fuck it," she whispered to herself and called on more magic, slightly blurring her image to anyone watching her. She hoped anyone who saw it could rationalize it away due to their state of panic.

Kate took in what she could, but there were pillars blocking about thirty percent of the front. What tables she could see were surrounded by empty seats. Some tables had people huddled together underneath them, but not as many as she'd expected. She hoped that meant most of the people had escaped during the chaos.

The second guy who had burst through the door stood next to someone crouching down or kneeling. There were too many tables in the way for Kate to figure out what exactly he was doing; only the top of his head was visible.

To the right of the two men were some people standing in a row, but they were too far away for her to know if they were magic. If it wasn't for the blast of magic the first guy threw, she wouldn't have known he was magic either.

The urge to stand up taller to see what was going on ate at her like a fierce itch that begged to be scratched.

At a tug on her jeans, she looked down.

Anything? Isabella threw the thought into her mind.

I can't tell what's happening. I'm going to listen.

Looking back at the front of the room, Kate sent some magic to her ears to enhance her hearing.

"What the fuck are you doing?" Standing Guy asked.

"Fuckin' relax, man. I just need to get the guy's wallet for ID to prove who he is."

A moment later, Crouching Man jumped to his feet and held up a wallet like it was a trophy before shoving it in his pocket. He nodded at Standing Guy, and they both walked over to the line of people.

Kate still couldn't tell how many people were in the line, but she could see four before her line of sight was cut off by a pillar. From the angle Crouching Man was facing, she expected there were at least a few more.

"You have a choice to make," Crouching Man directed to the group. "You come with us and serve Maverick, or you end up like him," he said as he half-turned and pointed to the floor behind him. Kate didn't need much brain power to know there was a dead body on the ground. It was likely the first guy who had run into the restaurant.

"Fuck you!" someone said.

"Your choice," Standing Guy said and raised his hand toward the line of people. A second later, a scream pierced the air.

"Shut the fuck up!" Crouching Man yelled, and the screaming stopped as if a switch had been flicked. "Now, we'll ask again. You can join Maverick or end up dead like these two fuckers. What will it be?"

Kate didn't wait to hear what they were going to choose. Ducking back under the table, she cut the extra power to her hearing. *They've got magics lined up.* She paused before sending another message as she was only able to send less than ten words at a time. *They're killing anyone who doesn't agree to join Maverick.*

Isabella grabbed Kate's arm and pulled, almost toppling her over. She managed to steady herself, and Isabella spoke right into her ear. "Repeat what I say."

What? Kate asked telepathically.

"Don't argue," Isabella whispered. "Just repeat what I say. It can't be done telepathically. Say the words."

Kate wasn't sure what Isabella was doing but nodded anyway.

"With these whispered words, a mystical defense is spun."

As soon as she heard the words, Kate knew that Isabella was giving her Reece's protection spell. She immediately repeated each line.

"Cloaked in safety by the moon and the sun.
Weave a shield, protect my frame."

Isabella paused. "Shit, I can't remember the next line. We'll just skip it and hope the rest is enough."

Figuring there wasn't much else they could do, Kate nodded for Isabella to continue.

"Shadows form, protect my being.
Safe from harm, danger freeing."

When Kate finished repeating the spell, she pushed some more power to her hearing to see if she could tell what was happening in the front of the restaurant.

"Check under the tables," one of the men said.

They were coming for them.

Flash. She threw the word into Isabella's mind with a sense of urgency.

With a nod, Isabella acknowledged that she heard her, but before Kate could do anything, their table disappeared.

The extra light that suddenly surrounded them froze Kate for a fraction of a second. Out of the corner of her eye, she saw Isabella disappear, and she pulled on her magic to do the same right as something clamped onto her arm.

Ignoring the hold on her arm, Kate tried to flash but nothing happened. The grip on her arm tightened.

"Not so fast, bitch." She turned her head to look at her captor. Standing Guy dragged her to the front of the room. "She's the last magic, but her friend got away," he said, pushing Kate toward a line of five people.

She reeled, stumbling forward and almost falling into a pillar before she straightened. It was then she saw four bodies on the floor.

Her entire world shrunk down to those lifeless bodies. Their eyes were closed like they were sleeping, but the gaping, charred holes in their torsos told the true story. A frisson of fear shot through Kate. It started at her toes and snaked upward until all she could feel was a sense of debilitating horror. A few minutes ago, those bodies had been people having dinner. Maybe laughing with a loved one. Was that going to be her fate too?

Somewhere in front of her, one of Maverick's minions said something. She looked at him but couldn't understand what he was saying. It felt like her fear had taken control of her senses. Her hearing felt like it shut down while her sight felt enhanced and ensured she didn't miss a single detail of the macabre sight before her. She saw it all, from the way their faces had paled when their life force had left them, to the torn and burnt skin like a distorted maw that once held the beating organs of a person just like her.

Wrenching back control of her senses, she tore her eyes from the bodies and looked over at the people in line. Something was wrong. They were standing as stiff as surfboards stuck in the sand. Their eyes were open but glazed over, as if unseeing what was in front of them.

Kate had already experienced robotic-like magics when they'd attacked her in her workshop a couple of weeks ago. This could be the same. Eddie was the only one of the group who hadn't been a zombie. Like the two goons in front of her.

Crouching Man moved in front of her but didn't touch her. "You have a choice to make," he said, repeating the words she'd heard him say to the people in the line. "You come with us and serve Maverick or you'll end up like them."

Kate didn't look where he pointed, the images of the bodies already imprinted in her mind. Something she would likely never forget. Looking him directly in the eyes, her choice was easy. She took a step back. If he touched her, he could block her magic like Standing Guy did before.

Not only did Kate not want to be a zombie, she was fucking sick and tired of men telling her what to do. She hated being bossed around. Being told what her choices were. And she hated being treated like she was less than.

Her apprenticeship gave her enough of that for several lifetimes. Years ago, she'd promised herself that no man would ever make a choice for her again.

Pulling as much energy from her surroundings as she could, she made her own choice. "Go fuck yourself!" she yelled.

"Your choice, bitch!" he said, and she flashed.

As she disappeared, a searing pain cut through her torso.

7

Isaac landed in the boardroom and quickly side-stepped to avoid knocking into Damon as the other man landed beside him.

Scanning the room, Isaac realized that the wall between the two large boardrooms had been removed since he'd last been there. Several of the council members had already arrived, as had some of the other regulars from the Williams's weekly family dinners. The place was filling up quickly.

Someone touched his arm, and he turned and noticed Isabella had come up beside him. "I'm so sorry," she said as she leaned into Reece, whose arm was around her shoulders.

Fear crawled up his spine and his stomach wanted to leap into his throat, but he forced down the panic. "For what?" he asked Isabella, hoping it was something like forgetting to tell him about a cupcake sale. He knew it wasn't, but he could hope.

Twice now he'd rushed to Kate's side because she'd been hurt, but he refused to think the worst.

"When I flashed out of the restaurant, I thought Kate was right behind me. She told me to go. I flashed here, but she didn't come. I should have waited, but she told me to go," Isabella repeated, and suddenly, she was wringing a small cloth between her fingers.

Isaac had seen her conjure a cloth the other day in his shop when she was upset. He rocked onto the balls of his feet, wanting to move as his fear grew. Each second that Isabella didn't get on with it felt like an eternity, but he plastered a pleasant look on his face and waited.

"Jack arrived with Meredith," Isabella finally continued. "We waited, and I kept expecting to see Kate. I was sure she would come any second." Isabella spoke in a rush, like if she pushed the words out quickly enough, everything would be alright. She continued to wind the cloth around her fingers until their tips went white.

Reece must have noticed as he laid one hand over Isabella's and gently loosened the cloth.

When Isabella didn't say anything more, Isaac opened his mouth to ask where Kate was when Reece spoke up. "Kate managed to flash here, but she was hurt," he said. "She's in the back of the room with Jack."

A part of Isaac wanted to rush to Kate and another part of him was afraid that seeing her hurt again would shred him.

While that war raged within him, he turned to Isabella. "Thank you for looking out for Kate."

She nodded and turned back into Reece's side.

Isaac knew there was only one choice for him to make, no matter how terrified he was. Turning around, he walked toward the back of the room. He didn't flash and he didn't rush, needing the time to calm himself. With a normal stride, he took in everything in front of him.

Kate lay on top of a table that was pushed against the wall. Jack was bent over her still form, his hands pressed against her skin, just above her waist. Fiona stood to the side, holding one of Kate's limp hands.

When Isaac was only a few feet away, he noticed Kate's shirt was charred and hanging open, exposing the skin just above her waist.

"Oh, Isaac, honey. Good thing you're here," Fiona said as she picked up his hand and put Kate's into it, before moving out of the way. On instinct, Isaac enclosed Kate's hand in both of his.

Careful not to disturb Jack, Isaac bent over Kate, pressing a kiss to her forehead. Her skin was cool against his lips. Instinctively, he pushed warmth into her.

"Thanks," Jack said, his head bowed and his eyes closed.

Isaac was continually surprised by Jack and thankful the strength of his magic could heal Kate.

Another eternity passed by in the next few minutes as Isaac waited for Jack to finish healing Kate. Then, like he'd done in her shop the week before, Jack passed his hand over Kate, and her eyes fluttered open.

"I'll give you two a minute," he said and walked away.

Fiona kissed Kate on the forehead. "Stop scaring me," she scolded her daughter, but there wasn't any heat in her words. She squeezed Isaac's shoulder and headed to the other side of the room.

"Oh, shit! Not again," Kate groaned as she pushed up onto her elbows and looked around the room.

Isaac felt as if he could read her thoughts in that moment, or maybe he just knew her well. Kate hated having the attention on her in what she would consider a moment of personal weakness. What she didn't realize was that she was anything but weak. Within the last three weeks, she'd been attacked twice, once brutally, and she'd had her mind controlled.

She slid off the table and started to keel to the left. He flung his hands out to steady her.

"Please," he said quietly as he moved in front of her and pushed her back until her butt rested on the edge of the table for support. "Please," he said again, his tone pleading. "Let me be here for you. I need to care for you. Will you allow me to do this right now?"

Her eyes met his, her face still pale. She opened her mouth and he feared she was going to reject him. Then she closed her mouth and made an almost imperceptible nod. He was almost afraid to think about how physically weak she must be if she was willing to give in so easily. He wanted to give her more than just physical support, but he'd take that for now.

Adopting the same position as her, leaning his ass on the edge of the table, he reached for her hips and gently guided her in front of him. When she leaned back on him, allowing him to hold her, he felt like he'd been given a gift. Loosely, he wrapped his arms around her, and she rested her hands on top of his.

"Thank you," he whispered quietly. She squeezed his hand in acknowledgment, and that was enough for now.

Finally looking at the others in the room, he saw all eyes were on them, something Kate hated. At least now there was something more he could do to help her.

"Isabella," he said, raising his voice above the soft din in the room. "Could you explain what happened?"

"Sure. Kate and I—"

"Isabella," Meredith said, interrupting, "before you get into it, why doesn't everyone grab a chair and get comfortable. As you can see, the two rooms have been joined and the chairs and tables pushed aside to make room for everyone to flash here. We didn't want anyone flashing on top of a table, but there's no need to be uncomfortable."

Isaac appreciated that Meredith made it possible for him to get Kate to sit without signaling her out.

Before he could even let go of Kate to get some chairs, Damon had brought two over. He gave Kate's shoulder a squeeze, perhaps a gesture he'd learned from their mother, but he didn't say anything. Something Isaac was happy about. In a moment, Kate would have more attention than she wanted.

There was some shuffling and moving about as tables and chairs were rearranged. It gave Isaac the perfect opportunity to get Kate off her feet. But instead of using the chairs Damon brought by, Isaac pushed a bit of magic into his legs and, using the extra strength, he hopped backward onto the table, pulling her with him.

She let out a small squeak as he rested his back against the wall and pulled her more firmly between his legs. He feared she would protest, but then she settled back into him.

Now he would just have to stay calm while he heard what had happened.

AT FIRST, Kate wondered what everyone would think about her sitting between Isaac's legs. Her face heated with shame at her weaknesses—first being hurt several times in as many weeks, and now letting Isaac support her.

Looking around the room, she wondered how many eyes were on her. To her surprise, there were none. All eyes were on Jack as he stood at the end of the long room, prepared to address the group, yet she couldn't help but notice the couples.

Reece had Isabella tucked into his side, Connor had his arms around Rowena, Jo and Simon were holding hands as they leaned against a wall, and the biggest surprise of all was her brother. Damon was sitting on the floor against a wall, and Morgana was sitting between his legs just like Kate was between Isaac's.

Her friends were already couples; would they assume she and Isaac were as well when they were merely sleeping together? She could set people straight on their relationship later.

Jack cleared his throat and all conversation in the room ceased. "Before Isabella and Kate explain what happened at the restaurant, I'd like to bring something else to your attention." Jack paused as Frank and Ben tended to do—maybe it was an FBI thing, to make sure people were listening. Then he looked at Kate's mom, and her mom nodded. Kate had no idea what that was about.

"Some of you may have heard that Fiona has had a recurring vision of Kate lying unconscious in a white room. I've also had some visions lately. In one, I was with several of you."

Now she knew why her mom nodded at Jack. Kate just hoped she wasn't in one of Jack's visions as well. She wasn't sure she'd be able to handle any more protectiveness.

"The recurring vision I've been having involves Meredith, Reece, and Morgana," Jack continued. "We're trapped in some kind of cave."

"Do you have an idea when it might happen?" Reece asked.

"Unfortunately, I didn't get a calendar invite," Jack said, and there were a few chuckles in the room. It wasn't often that Kate heard Jack crack a joke. "But... the visions I've had in the last two years have come to fruition within one to two months of when I first get them."

"Jack. You'll let us know more as soon as you know," Damon said. So like her brother; Kate knew he was making a statement and not asking a question.

Jack nodded. "Of course... Now, Isabella, would you mind walking us through what happened tonight?"

Kate listened but didn't interject as Isabella covered everything. She couldn't have known exactly what had happened to Kate once she was alone, but Isabella got the gist of it.

When Isabella was finished and had answered a few questions from the group, Jack turned to Kate. "Anything to add?"

Kate shook her head.

"Okay, then I'd like to—" Jack stopped talking when Frank and Ben arrived in the middle of the room.

Both men had been like fathers to Kate since her own

father had died, but now, as she looked at the expressions on their faces and their suits, there wasn't anything fatherly about them. They were in pure FBI mode.

Jack asked Frank and Ben to fill the group in on what they'd learned.

Like Jack had, Frank walked to the end of the room and waited until all eyes were on him.

"Ben and I just came from an emergency meeting and learned that the Secretary of the Department of Health and Human Services has declared a nationwide public health emergency. The magics in the organization who we spoke with believe Maverick has created some kind of enslaving spell that is quickly being spread by his minions. There have been reports from each state, as well as from Canadian cities closest to our borders."

"That sounds exactly like what Isabella explained she and Kate witnessed," Jack interjected. "What do the non-magics believe it is?"

"They think it's a virus and are shutting down all public facilities, along with ordering schools to close and hospitals to be on lockdown. We've already seen that Maverick can only control magics, but since the non-magic authorities are not aware of this, it is creating a panic unlike anything we've ever seen before."

Ben stepped forward. "Jack. Are you and your council any closer to finding a way to extract the evil from Maverick?"

"We're bouncing some theories around right now." Jack turned to Ben's daughter. "Sam? You care to comment?"

Sam didn't step forward, but she didn't cower either.

"Not yet. I need more time before I come to you with a plan. A few days to a week, maybe."

Frank smiled at his niece before turning back to Jack. "Then you've got about a week to figure out what to do with the sword and how to close the box."

Kate felt Isaac stiffen against her back.

8

Isaac hated what was coming. He would be forced to make a decision he had promised himself he would never make again. And regardless of the decision he made, he was fucked.

If he agreed to tattoo Kate, he risked killing her. And if he didn't agree and she couldn't work with the sword, at least thousands would die. If anyone else presented him with such a problem, he would say the answer was easy—the many over the one. But then, their one wasn't Kate.

"Isaac?" Jack asked. The silence in the room was deafening as everyone focused on him.

Knowing he was going to piss off Kate, Isaac had to ask the questions on his mind anyway. He cared more about her safety than whether she was angry with him.

"When I tested to see if I could give Kate the protective tattoo, I didn't like the pushback I got. It could be dangerous for her."

Isaac felt Kate sit up straighter, putting a few inches between their bodies, but he forged ahead. "I know Kate is a skilled swordsmith, but is there no one else who can forge the lock?"

Kate didn't say a word as she scrambled off the table and leaned against the wall. It was better than her stomping out of the room, but not by much.

Since he didn't have Kate in front of him anymore, he slid off the table as well. Isaac bet on Kate's desire not to make a scene and took the risk by going over to her. He casually adopted her position and leaned against the wall. If she pulled away now, she would draw more attention to herself.

When Kate stayed where she was, he was thankful he'd taken his own bet.

Jack waited until Isaac settled before he spoke. "While I had the sword, I decided to run a few tests." He held up his hand toward Kate. "And before you say anything, Kate, I had to look at the problem from all angles."

In his peripheral vision, Isaac saw Kate nod, which Jack must have taken as acquiescence. If he did, he didn't know Kate very well, but it didn't matter; the outcome was still the same.

Jack turned so he was once more addressing everyone in the room. "I had Kate's old mentor, Henry, inspect the sword. Henry is magic, and I explained the risk to him before presenting the sword. He laid one hand on the sword and collapsed into unconsciousness. Once I revived him, he was fine, but obviously that means he can't help, and I expect Kate is the only magic swordsmith who can because of her ability to feel emotions in objects."

Isaac expected that if he was looking at Kate, he would see a smug look on her face, but he wasn't ready to give up yet. "Jack? What about a non-magic swordsmith?"

"I tried that too. Henry asked two of his former apprentices to look at the sword. They could both pick it up, but when they did, the sword disguised itself. The intricate designs that Henry and I could both clearly see disappeared when the non-magics touched it."

Jack paused, as if he wanted to let the information sink in with Isaac before he continued. "I also had Reece look for a spell that might protect Kate instead of having to rely on a tattoo. Unfortunately, they all seemed to be generic to protect against outside forces. They might work, but if Kate is touching the sword and it has her body attack her from the inside, a spell wouldn't be enough. Your tattoo has the best chance of protecting her since your magic would be embedded into her."

Isaac expected Jack knew Isaac no longer had a choice and was waiting for him to admit it.

Hoping he wasn't sending Kate to her death, Isaac addressed Jack. "I'll tattoo the protection onto Kate." Just the thought of agreeing to something that held such a high risk made him uncomfortable. He just couldn't see another way.

Jack nodded and turned back to the group with some last-minute instructions about working with Sam on a solution.

A few minutes later, the meeting broke up, and one by one, people flashed away or walked out the door.

Isaac was surprised when Kate came to stand in front of him. He'd expected her to leave without saying a word to him.

"You don't trust me, Isaac. Without trust, there can't be a relationship between us, regardless of whether or not you care. I'll be at your shop at nine tomorrow morning."

She flashed away before Isaac could say a word. Now the only person remaining in the room, he didn't move. Leaning against the wall, he closed his eyes and wondered how he could avoid giving Kate the same fate he had given his brother.

9

By the time Kate made it back to her house, she felt like she'd been awake for a week. Certain sleep would come quickly, she crawled into bed and prepared to let the day fall away.

And it may have if Isaac's look of disappointment wasn't etched into her mind like permanent ink. When he agreed to give her the tattoo only because he was being shoved into a corner, it felt like all the work she'd done over the years to prove herself had been for naught. Isaac didn't trust her.

He wasn't going to give her the tattoo because he believed she was skilled and had a job to do or because he trusted her to know what she needed. No, it was because Jack had pushed him into a corner.

Maybe that wasn't fair. There were many events that had contributed to Isaac's decision, not just Jack's request. But even the circumstances couldn't lessen the bitter resentment she felt at the lack of Isaac's trust. Which meant he didn't respect her either.

After he showed up at her place the other night, she thought maybe he was coming around. Instead, he was turning out to be like all the other men she'd met—family and closest friends notwithstanding—who used women.

Kate knew her logic was flawed. She was the one using him for his body since she wanted no-strings sex. But if he had really wanted more, wouldn't he have pushed for it?

She was so confused. For years, she'd been so sure that casual sex was all she should ever want from a man. Then Isaac happened. He talked the talk, saying he wanted more from her. That he cared for her. Well, in her book, relationships were supposed to be an equal amount of give and take. But as soon as Kate needed something from him, he pulled back. If he cared so deeply about her, wouldn't he have understood how much her career meant to her? Wouldn't he have wanted to help her in any way he could?

It wasn't just that forging the sword would help the magic world; it would mean that her skill had helped. Her, Kate Stone, who her ex-fiancé said wasn't good enough because she was a woman. If Isaac had wanted to give her the tattoo to help her, it would say he respected her skills and her as a person.

Being able to work with the sword and help contain the evil would mean no one would ever again be able to say she wasn't good enough. That she couldn't do what a man could.

After stewing over Isaac and tossing and turning for what felt like hours, Kate forced all thoughts of him from her mind. When she met with him in the morning, she needed to be strong and not show him how much he'd hurt her. For that, she needed sleep.

Lying on the bed, she took a deep breath and forced her mind to go blank, then closed her eyes. At first, it worked, and her body relaxed and she sunk deeper into the mattress.

Then images of the dead people on the restaurant floor swam before her mind's eye. She remembered the terror she'd felt, how it had snaked up her spine and taken hold.

Instead of trying to push the images aside, Kate chose to replace them. She visualized the sword. Next, she imagined herself working with it, seeing her fire manipulate the magical metal. It would work for a few minutes. Then visions of the bodies crowded back into her mind, and she would start all over again with visualizing the sword.

It became a never-ending cycle until exhaustion finally won out. Sometime in the early hours of the morning, she must have fallen asleep.

The dream started just as the scene had played out in the restaurant. Then it morphed, as most dreams did.

Dream Kate tried to look away from the bodies on the floor, but something tugged at her leg. She looked down, and one of the bodies, its eyes now wide open, had pitched itself closer to her. Its body distorted with the movement as its hand firmly grasped Dream Kate's ankle. She screamed and jerked her leg, trying to step back, as terror paralyzed her.

Another body inched forward and grabbed her other leg. Continuing to jerk and pull herself away, she yelled at the bodies. She couldn't kick them because their grip on her was too tight, squeezing her flesh like it was clamped in a vice until she thought her bones would break.

Dream Kate was tiring quickly. When they tugged on her leg again, she looked down. The remaining bodies had their eyes open and began to chant, "Help me." Their voices sounded hollow and surreal as they chanted the plea over and over again.

"This is your fault," Crouching Man said. "If you had flashed when Isabella told you to, she wouldn't be dead."

Confused by his comment, Kate looked to where he pointed and tried to scream, but no sound emerged.

Kate's own scream pulled her from the dream. She was panting like she'd sprinted a marathon, her throat dry and scratchy. The image of Isabella on the floor, a charred hole in her chest as she pleaded for help, was fresh in Kate's mind.

She turned her head to read the clock on her nightstand and then flopped back on the bed. "Ugh," she mumbled. Only six—still three hours before she had to meet Isaac at his shop.

Too afraid to sleep now, she threw off the covers, got out of bed, and trudged to the bathroom. Maybe a shower would help clear the haunting images from her mind.

An hour later, showered and dressed, Kate sat at her kitchen table, sipping her third cup of coffee. When she tried to eat something, her stomach revolted, images from her dream taunting her. Coffee would have to do.

Trying not to think about the dream, Kate rehashed everything that was said in the boardroom the night before. That turned out to be a bad idea.

By the time she arrived at Isaac's shop, past feelings of

inadequacy were driving her and she was ready for a fight.

"I'm working on the design," Isaac said in way of greeting.

"Okay." She sat on a tattoo chair and stared at his back.

Fifteen minutes passed without either of them saying a word. She watched the clock, and each round of the minute hand cranked her anger higher, as if the clock had a direct link to her emotions.

All the times she had worked so hard to prove herself as a swordsmith but was dismissed by her peers because she was a woman ran through her mind. She thought of the sexist comments and ridicule she'd endured because she didn't have a dick.

"If I were a man, you wouldn't hesitate to give me the tattoo," she said to Isaac's back. "No one would have to force you." As soon as the words left her mouth, she realized she hadn't really meant the words for Isaac. They had been for every man in her past who hadn't trusted or respected her. Isaac was just the lucky guy who was hearing them.

He turned on his stool and lifted his gaze to hers. A frown marred his forehead, his eyes narrowed in anger. His expression told her she had gone too far.

KATE'S WORDS had been clear, and yet Isaac had trouble believing what he'd heard. He stood but didn't utter a single word, too stunned by her accusation to respond.

Staring into her eyes, he waited a moment, hoping his

brain would shift back into gear and give him a reasonable way to respond. He opened his mouth, then shut it again.

Her comment had cut deep. Not because of the actual words, per se, but because they revealed her true feelings about him. She believed his decision was based on some farfetched idea that he didn't see her as an equal.

What she really should have seen was how much he cared for her and that he wasn't willing to risk hurting her. That's what hurt the most. She still couldn't see what he felt for her.

He wanted to set her straight. To confess his feelings and have her respond in kind. Though he knew she wouldn't. She was too scared to admit that she cared. And as long as she was in denial about her feelings, she would twist anything he said to fit into the lies she had told herself.

Kate was looking for a fight and she had been since the moment she walked into his shop. She might believe she had kept herself emotionally distanced from him over the last year, but he knew better. If he spoke now, not only would she twist his words, he might respond in a way he would regret later.

"I need a minute," he said as he pushed by her, on his way to the restroom. Kate had a habit of running away, and since he had confronted her on it, he couldn't do the same, but he still needed a moment to collect himself.

"Isaac, wait—"

He turned around and saw the worry, and perhaps regret, etched on her face. Last week, he had made the promise that he would be there for her to lean on. That meant he couldn't leave as soon as she said something he didn't like. "I'm not going anywhere, Kate. I just need a minute, okay?"

When she nodded, he walked to the restroom. Once inside, he closed the door and leaned back against it, closing his eyes. *If I were a man.* Her words ran on repeat in his mind.

Not once in his entire life had he ever disrespected a woman or thought of her as less. From the first moment he had met Kate, she had his respect. More than that—she had his admiration. He'd been so impressed by her drive and strength to seek out a career in a field that was traditionally a man's domain. She was talented and strong. Caring and loyal to her friends and family. Beautiful inside and out, even if she didn't like showing him her vulnerability.

Kate was the main reason Isaac had taken Meredith up on her offer of a rental space. It had been time to leave Oregon, to find a place to start over, and Blue Mountain had far more to offer him than just that. Even more than a great location for a shop and a found-family ready to include him, it had Kate.

It hadn't taken him long to see the chip on her shoulder, although he hadn't known what had put it there. Yet it didn't worry him. So, when she had offered a friends-with-benefits arrangement, he took her up on her offer. Even though he knew he would want more eventually. He was a patient man; he was willing to take his time and show Kate what they could have together.

If I were a man. "Fuck," he muttered quietly. He wanted to be mad at her for saying those words, but he wasn't. Sure, they hurt, but he shouldn't have been surprised by them. His patience and his willingness to let Kate set the pace of their relationship meant they hadn't gotten to know each other as well as they should have.

Never once had he explained what had happened in his past and how he approached his magic. That was on him. Now he had to figure out how to fix it.

He left the restroom and walked back into the room they had been using, worried she might be gone.

He found her pacing back and forth in the small space. The fact that she hadn't left told him they could work things out. He was under no delusions that it would be easy. Only that it was possible.

"Kate," he said her name softly as he walked into the room, prepared for her passionate explosion.

10

*H*oly fuck! What the hell had she been thinking? She hadn't been, that much was obvious. She'd let all the events of yesterday, a sleepless night, a nightmare, and thoughts of the past confuse her, and she had taken it out on someone who didn't deserve it.

"Kate."

She turned toward the door when Isaac said her name.

"Isaac… I didn't mean…" She wanted to finish but couldn't. How could she explain? Everything that happened had messed her up so much that she was projecting all her hurt and shit onto Isaac.

She should leave. She was already forcing him to do something he didn't want to do, and now she'd hurt him deeply with her careless accusations. Words she'd spewed because she was taking out her fear and shame on him.

Maybe she was the coward he had accused her of being.

If that was true, then getting the tattoo so she could

work with the sword was an opportunity to prove herself once and for all. Once that was done, she could maybe let herself care for Isaac. Be vulnerable with him.

Too bad it all came back to needing Isaac's help. Now she wasn't so sure she deserved it. At least not yet. If she took a day or two to get a grip on her emotions, maybe she could figure out a way to apologize.

There would still be the matter of him not wanting to give her the tattoo… But one thing at a time.

"I think I should go."

Before she could flash, Isaac gently gripped her upper arm. "Look, Kate—"

A thunderous blast shook the building.

Kate stumbled, instinctively flinging her arms out to find purchase. Isaac wrapped his arms around her, both of them rocking to the side until he steadied them. "What was that?" she asked as they both rushed to the main area of the shop. She looked around as if the shop could give her answers.

"It sounded like it came from next door. We should—"

"Oh my god, The Magic Plate! We need to check to make sure everyone's okay." Kate tried to pull away from Isaac, but he tightened his grip.

"Wait!" He moved one hand to her cheek, and she wanted to turn into his touch but met his gaze instead. "We don't know what happened. Maverick is creating fucking havoc everywhere. This could be a trap."

"The restaurant," she whispered as she visualized the restaurant from the night before. Then she saw the version of Isabella from her dream as clear as day in her mind. Her friend with a gaping hole in her chest, begging Kate for help. A cold shiver snaked down her spine, and she felt her world shrink as it had the night before—terror freezing her where she stood.

Isaac's thumb rubbed along her cheek, bringing her back to the present. "We don't know if anything like that has happened. Let me reach out to Reece to see what he knows. He'll at least be able to tell us if only the middle building was affected."

Kate felt the air drift across her cheek from the absence of Isaac's hand. His small touch shouldn't mean so much; maybe she only needed comfort because of the moment.

Isaac pulled his phone from his pocket just as another rumble detonated through the building, followed by dozens of screams.

The force of the blast chucked her forward, sending her crashing into Isaac, his phone flinging into the air behind them.

Momentum carried them forward, smashing them into one of the empty tattoo stations. Kate smacked her head as they knocked into a portable worktable, toppling it to the floor.

They skidded along the floor, colliding into two more stations. Metal clanged against metal as portable carts and trays crashed to the floor ahead of Kate and Isaac as they finally came to a stop.

Before Kate could take stock of all that had happened, Isaac was pulling her to her feet. His hands ran down her arms. "Are you hurt? All I can sense is a bump on your head," he said, his voice sounding shaky.

Kate gently prodded her temple with her fingers and only felt a slight bit of pain. "I'm fine. What about you?"

"I'm good. But I'm also not the one who almost died

last night." He leaned down and kissed her softly on the lips, but he had already straightened before she had time to react. "You've had more than your fair share of knocks and injuries lately."

She let out a shaky laugh. "I guess I have. I—" She felt something soft on her face and rubbed her cheek. Her fingers came away white. "What's that?" she while looking up. The panels from the drop ceiling had come loose.

"I'm thinking whatever rocked the other building did some damage in here."

Kate followed Isaac's gaze as he looked around his shop. Dust and plaster floated in the air, and ceiling tiles covered the couch in the sitting area. Books and framed drawings littered the floor, along with pieces of several workstations.

It was then the absence of sound struck her. "There's no screaming," she whispered, not even trying to disguise the fear in her voice. "Last night… there'd been so much noise as people scrambled about, and then it got quiet. Eerily quiet." She rubbed her hands up and down her arms and sent a small blast of magic throughout her system to combat the sudden chill and looked up at Isaac. "If anything happened, we're to flash to the boardroom, like I did last night."

Isaac's gaze was soft as it met hers. "Yes, but the board-room is in the first building, and even if none of the blasts were there, they could have affected its structural integrity."

Kate could read between the lines and knew what he wasn't saying. If there was structural damage, there could be casualties as well.

"Can you try Reece again?" she asked, not only

because she wanted to find out what was going on but because she needed reassurance that her friends were okay.

"I don't have my phone." He looked around the room as if he could locate it in the mess.

"It's okay, I've got mine." Kate reached around to her back pocket when a telepathic message entered her mind. *An update.*

Isaac nodded to let her know that he got Jack's message too.

They didn't have to wait long before Jack continued.

Buildings attacked. Stay where you are. Help coming to you.

That didn't tell them much, and now Kate was even more worried. Jack said the buildings were attacked, but she and Isaac hadn't seen anyone yet. That could mean that all the apartments above them had been threatened or besieged.

Incoming. Kate heard Jack's voice a moment before Ben and his daughter, Sam, flashed into the front of the shop.

"You both okay?" Ben asked as they walked toward each other, meeting in the middle of the shop.

"We're good. It's just me and Kate here. Can we help somewhere?"

Ben shook his head. "Jack has the rest of the buildings covered. No one was seriously hurt, just minor injuries from falling debris."

"My shop and the bakery are the only businesses in the buildings open right now, so there can't be many people around."

"Then we got lucky, but Maverick is up to something and likely wanted to make a distraction, or he would have done more damage." Sam said.

"You're thinking it was a distraction to get to Kate?" Isaac asked.

Kate jerked her gaze to Isaac. "But I don't have the sword. Jack does."

"Not right now, you don't. But it doesn't mean you won't soon. Plus, Maverick might not know that," Ben said. "Unfortunately, Sam had a lot of opportunity to study Maverick…" Ben's voice cracked and his eyes became glassy with moisture.

Sam leaned into her dad, wrapping an arm around his waist and giving him a quick hug. "It's okay, Dad," Sam whispered, but it was loud enough for Kate to hear, and probably Isaac too.

"We can't underestimate Maverick," Sam said when she faced the again. "I don't believe he had a conscious, even before he consumed what was in the box. He's an extreme narcissist, believing he should have whatever he wants, and he refuses to let anything stand in his way. So, my guess is, whether or not he thinks you have the sword, he knows you have the ability to forge it into something else, so he'll come for you."

Ben nodded at his daughter. "I believe Sam is right," Ben said, his eyes now clear and focused. "Once the council members and those working with us have secured the other buildings, we'll come up with a plan."

"That won't be necessary, Ben," a deep, Darth Vader-like voice said from behind them.

All four of them spun to see a man's feet touch down on the floor after his voice reached them.

Kate hadn't seen Maverick, real name Forest Sharpe, since she was little, but her gut was telling her the man in front of her was him. He'd been a council leader with her father. Maverick didn't look much different than she expected, just older. If she'd met him on the street, she would think he was someone's nice grandfather. But looks could be deceiving.

Damon had told her that Maverick and his cohorts were responsible for her father's death. They had also been responsible for stealing children and faking their deaths. Kate briefly struggled with reconciling knowing what she did and seeing the ordinary-looking older man in front of her. But evil and hatred could come in all forms. She had learned that the hard way.

"Your protection spells are amusing but not even worth the magic it took to cast them." He walked closer, a smile on his face like he was greeting old friends. "How are you feeling, Ben? Recovered from your little incident in Mexico? I see you've gotten acquainted with your daughter again after you abandoned her for more than twenty years."

Kate could hear the taunts in Maverick's voice. When Ben took a step forward, she sucked in her breath, fearing what was to come.

She pulled in energy around her and pushed magic into her fingertips, unsure what to do but wanting to be ready.

Maverick lifted his chain, his gaze locking on hers. "Oh, Kate. You're so cute, thinking that charging your measly magic will help you. If I want something, I'll take it. Right, Ben?" he jeered.

As Kate watched, her magic still tingling and ready in her fingers, something happened to Maverick's face. His cheek pushed out on one side as if someone had pinched the skin and pulled. Just as quickly, the bulge disappeared, and one appeared in his neck before it too vanished.

"What do you want, Maverick?" Ben asked. "Or maybe you're here to brag. You always were an arrogant asshole. I see nothing has changed."

"And you always were a self-righteous bastard, Ben." Maverick smiled, his teeth looking Hollywood-white. "And as for what I want?" He grinned wider. "I'm here to have some fun." Maverick raised his hand above his head, snapped his fingers, and the entire building rocked.

WHEN MAVERICK RAISED his arm above his head, Isaac knew something bad was about to happen, even before Maverick snapped his fingers.

Isaac reached for Kate, tugging her against him as the snap of Maverick's fingers reverberated through Ink Magic with the sound of a million fingers snapping at once. The building shook, and Isaac took Kate to the ground with him, shielding her body with his. The action was becoming all too familiar, and he feared that eventually it wouldn't be enough to protect her.

When something hit him in the back, he erected a magic bubble around them. It wouldn't be enough to save them if the building came down, but it would protect them against falling debris.

"How's that for fun, Ben?" Maverick asked, his voice carrying over the sounds of shouts and banging coming from the other buildings.

Isaac shifted off Kate and disintegrated the bubble. "You okay?" he whispered.

When she nodded, he helped her stand and saw that Sam and Ben seemed to be okay as well.

"Not my kind of fun," Ben told Maverick. "Just tell us what the fuck you want, Maverick, and then you can go on your merry way."

Maverick's face contorted; a portion of his cheek bulged out, and then another. "Stop!" he shouted, frantically looking around the room. "Shut the fuck up!"

A new sense of dread settled over Isaac. None of them had spoken a word. Something was happening to the man, and it didn't look like Maverick was in control of himself.

As if pulled by a string, Maverick jerked his face forward to face them. Then his gaze locked on Ben. "Kate has become a pain in my ass. Just like her father!"

Kate gasped from beside him, and he moved closer to her.

"You remember Curtis, don't you, Ben?" Maverick continued, but his jovial demeanor was now nowhere to be seen. "Curtis thought he could stop my plans to control all magics. He believed he was better than me right until his dying breath."

"That's because Curtis was a good man," Ben said, likely trying to distract Maverick as Ben took a step forward and closer to his daughter. "Something you never were, Maverick. Oh… and by the way, Maverick is such a stupid name. You're no Maverick; you're just a follower. You were always one of Daniel Knight's minions just like Copeland and Snake were. The council leader had all three of you dancing to his tune." As Ben continued to talk, he took three more steps sideways until he was blocking Maverick's direct line of sight to Sam.

"I was never a minion," Maverick spit out.

Ben's taunting had gotten to the man. It seemed he was good at dishing it out but not taking it. As Maverick continued to rant, Isaac copied Ben and moved over in front of Kate.

Isaac was willing to protect Kate with his life. Glancing around his shop, he realized that it just might come down to that. From the sounds of the shouting in the other buildings, it didn't seem like anyone would be coming to their rescue. It was only the four of them, and as independent and strong as Kate was, he would do everything in his power to make sure she was safe. Regardless of their recent argument, he cared more for her than he'd ever cared for anyone.

"I bet you would make a fucking fantastic minion, Ben, since you've been following rules all your life."

Isaac listened with half an ear to the taunts that Maverick and Ben continued to throw back and forth. It was then that two truths struck Isaac like a battering ram. One: if he had tattooed Kate when Damon had first mentioned it, she might not have been injured last night and could possibly be protected against whatever Maverick came at them with now. Maybe Kate was right, and Isaac hadn't trusted her. But it had nothing to do with her being a woman. She was wrong about that part.

The second truth was that Isaac had made a strategic error when he had copied Ben's actions. Kate was now standing behind him, and Isaac couldn't see her if she stepped to the side, or if Maverick flashed behind them.

"Nice chat, Ben," Maverick said, once more in a

friendly voice like he had come for tea. "Now, I really must get on with what I came to do. But I think I'll alter my plans slightly. At first, I thought I'd just kill Curtis's daughter, but now I think I'll add a twist to it."

As Maverick finished his sentence, Isaac saw the gleam in the man's eyes and he spun around toward Kate. As Isaac reached for her, a blast of magic hit her from the side, sending her flying backward.

Isaac lunged forward, using his magic to propel himself faster. He grabbed Kate's ankle just as the wall behind her opened, revealing a black void, and they were both sucked through the gaping hole.

A bitter cold slapped at Isaac while air pummeled them. It pulled at them and whipped their clothing around them, threatening to rip Kate from his hold.

Isaac fought against the wind and pushed his other hand forward, fighting against the gale forces. After what felt like minutes but was probably only seconds, his arm started to tire and he caught Kate's other ankle in his grip.

"Kate!" he yelled as they were dragged through the blackness. He held on to her with every ounce of strength he possessed.

The wind battered him from all sides and his legs flailed behind him. Isaac feared Kate was unconscious, but the tingling of his magic through his palms told him she was at least still alive.

For so long after his brother's death, he wondered if his magic specialty was a curse. Now, he knew it for the gift it was because he could feel Kate's living essence.

He didn't know how long they were hurled through the black abyss. Isaac lost all sense of time, holding onto Kate his only focus. His fingers had long since gone numb, and the only thing that kept him holding on was the feeling of Kate's life force through his palms.

Without warning, the current around him slowed down, and they began to drop.

He wouldn't have thought anything could be worse than being hurled through the cold darkness with Kate ahead of him and unconscious.

But Isaac was wrong. A new fear crawled through him. They were falling fast, and he had no idea what lay below them.

The darkness surrounding them was impenetrable, not a single point of light shining through. They could have miles left to fall or only a few feet. He had to figure out how to stop Kate's unconscious body from smacking into whatever they would hit.

As they continued to fall and the air lessened its force, Isaac knew he was running out of time.

Using all the strength he had left, he jerked Kate's legs toward him, forcing his arms down toward his knees. When her body came alongside his, he let go of one of Kate's legs. His fingers were stiff, but he didn't have time to loosen them up as he flung his arm around her torso. As quick as he could, he did the same with his other hand.

Still falling toward who the fuck knew what, Isaac let a breath escape him. Finally having Kate secured against his body made him breathe just a bit easier.

Flipping them over in the air so that Kate now lay prone on top of him, he hoped it would be enough.

11

Isaac noticed the change in the wind first. It no longer whipped around them at quite the same speed. Then the air became warmer. Not warm like in a home, but not the frigid cold it had been.

Their downward trajectory slowed again as if they were floating now instead of falling. Fisting Kate's shirt with one hand so he had a firm grip on her, he let go with his other. Pushing his free hand below him to feel something—anything—he waited, hoping it would be a solid surface.

A moment later, his fingers touched wood, and then his arm folded as he hit the floor, Kate's weight collapsing on top of him.

A loud bang echoed through the space.

Isaac flung his other arm back around Kate and protected her head with his hands as best he could.

Holding his breath, he waited for the other shoe to drop. Then barked out a laugh as he realized what he'd been thinking. No shoes, but he and Kate had dropped. A long fucking way.

They were lying on a hard floor, but wherever they were was as pitch black as the abyss they had fallen through. The space had warmed up some, but it still didn't feel a hell of a lot warmer than the fifty degrees it had been outside in Blue Mountain that morning.

Isaac closed his eyes so he was no longer straining them to try and see into the darkness and continued to hold onto Kate. He breathed in her scent as they lay still, the familiar smell calming him. Running his hands along her back and soaking in her reassuring essence through his palms, her heart beating against his chest, helped his own heartbeat slow.

After a few minutes of complete silence, he stuck out one hand and pulled on his magic. A small ball of light glowed in his palm. Laughter bubbled out of him at the relief that his magic worked.

Picturing Jack in his mind, Isaac reached out telepathically.

Jack?

After several tries and no response, Isaac reached out to Meredith. Same result—nothing.

Since his magic worked, even if he couldn't reach anyone, there was a chance he might be able to flash out of the room. The big question was whether or not he would be able to get back into it. Or if he could even figure out where the room was after he flashed. He decided he couldn't risk it and wouldn't flash until Kate was awake.

Laying the light ball on the floor, he used one hand, with a little help from his magic, to push into a sitting position. Cradling Kate in his lap with one arm around her back and her head against his shoulder, he picked up the light.

Slowly, he moved his palm in an arc, checking out their surroundings. The space seemed small and empty. When he sent his magic out into the room, he didn't sense anything living and figured they were safe.

Moving Kate carefully, he laid her on the floor and conjured a pillow and blanket because of the chill in the air. When she was as comfortable as he could make her, he stood with the light in his hand.

After pacing the distance in the room, he guessed it to be ten-by-ten feet. He could touch the ceiling without straightening out his arm, making it less than six and a half feet high.

Both the walls and the ceiling felt like plaster or drywall. They were smooth and cool to the touch.

Using his ball of light, he explored each corner of the room as well as the seams along the floor and ceiling. He couldn't find a single crack in the entire space, nor a door or window.

They were in a box.

But there was air. He couldn't find the source, but he could feel a light current, bringing the chill with it. The cold he could handle because it meant they wouldn't suffocate.

With nothing left to check, he conjured two lanterns and set them on the floor, one at each end of a wall. Next, he conjured a large mattress and some more blankets, as well as some bottles of water.

He knelt beside Kate and gently ran his hand over her cheek. Her skin was a bit cool to the touch, but he figured the temperature of the room could account for that. "Kate? Kate, can you hear me? Wake up, baby. I need to see your beautiful brown eyes."

She didn't even stir, and Isaac pushed down his panic. As long as he continued to feel her essence and her breathing seemed fine, he would stay calm. "It's okay, baby. You sleep as long as you want," he whispered.

Picking her up, he cradled her in his arms and carried her over to the bed. Positioning her head on a pillow, he laid down next to her, his chest against her back, and pulled her in close.

Now that they were safe, at least temporarily, Isaac rehashed what had happened in his shop. He didn't know if the explosions they'd heard from the other buildings were only distractions or if they had a bigger purpose.

If anyone had been pushed to choose between the options Kate told them about from the restaurant, he hoped that all chose the zombie route. At least that way they would still be alive. Isaac couldn't see how they could possibly reverse the mind control, but somehow, Jack and the rest of the council would find a way.

Staying positive, he looked on the bright side—at least he and Kate had escaped the zombie-fication. Only time would tell whether they were better off being locked in a box.

As to why they were in a box, only Maverick knew the answer to that. He'd said he wanted to kill Kate, and then said that he would add a twist. Isaac figured the box was the twist, and he hoped it wasn't a slow death from captivity.

If that was the case, it didn't make much sense. Isaac had never met Maverick before today, but he'd heard plenty of stories about him. Sending Kate to die in a box all alone wouldn't serve a purpose. He wouldn't get to see Kate suffer and wouldn't even be able to taunt her about her approaching death or use it as leverage for something else he could want.

Isaac shuddered at the thought of either one and pulled Kate more snuggly against him, more for his own reassurance than hers.

Pushing the thoughts to the side, Isaac focused on his next steps.

He would wait for Kate to wake up. Then they would try to flash out of there. If that didn't work, they would wait for someone to find them.

Ben and Sam had seen what happened; they would know to start a search. Isaac had faith in his friends. They would find them.

KATE FELT a hand running through her hair and knew instantly that it was Isaac. "Morning," she mumbled as she pushed her body closer to his warmth.

Isaac kissed the side of her face softly. "Hey, beautiful. That is the best sound I've ever heard. I'm so happy you're awake."

"Did you let me sleep in?" Kate turned over to face him and pushed up on her elbow.

They weren't in his bedroom or hers. The room's walls looked like a light color in the semi-darkness. The only light came from two lanterns against the wall opposite them.

Using Isaac as leverage, Kate pulled herself into a sitting position. What she'd first thought was a bed was only a mattress on the floor, and Isaac was leaning against the wall.

"Where are we?"

His eyes scanned her face, and he seemed hesitant before he spoke. "Do you remember being in my shop?"

She felt her face heat as shame consumed her. She'd yelled at him, accusing him of some awful things. "I'm so sorry," she whispered as she looked into his eyes. Her insecurities had made her speak the way she had. The fact their friends-with-benefits arrangement might be turning into so much more didn't give her the right to take out her anxiety on Isaac.

He cupped his large hand around the back of her neck and drew her to him. When he kissed her like there wouldn't be a tomorrow, she responded from somewhere deep in her soul, shoving her anxiety aside. They were both breathing heavily when he pulled back.

"It's okay. We can talk about all that stuff later. Can you remember what happened after we argued?"

Thinking back, she remembered she was going to walk out. Then the memories came flooding back with the force of a tsunami. "The building shook… Oh my god! Maverick came. First Ben and Sam and then Maverick, and there were explosions in the other buildings."

Isaac nodded and dropped his hand from her neck, waiting as she ran through her memories again.

"He admitted to killing my father. Then he said he was going to kill me, but he was going to add a twist to it?" She posed her words as a question, not sure she could trust her memory.

"That's right. Do you remember anything else?"

Kate searched her memories again, willing herself to remember. "Nothing," she said, shaking her head. "What happened? And you never did answer my other question —where are we?"

"We're in a room."

"Ha ha, funny guy. I figured that out for myself."

Kate waited for Isaac to smile and give her the punch line, but his expression remained serious. "Where is this room?" she asked quietly.

"I don't know." Isaac ran his hands through his hair and leaned his head back against the wall. "Maverick hit you with something. Not like a blast of magic, because you weren't injured. Well… you were unconscious. His blast opened up a hole in the wall."

"Like onto the street?" She tried to picture where he could have pushed them so they would end up in a room and she came up blank.

"A hole in the wall, but not to the outside." He shook his head. "Yes, to the outside… I think… but not onto the street. It was like a black hole opened up in the wall, but not like the night sky. It was pitch black."

"I remember Jo and Simon explaining how a hole opened up in the library wall and the book they needed was floating there." When she'd heard the story, she had pictured something like out of a fairytale, with lights and colors and maybe even vines surrounding the book. It had seemed beautiful and magical. But not magical in the way they had magic. Magical like a Disney story.

He nodded. "I remember. Rowena and Connor said they had a similar experience when they found the key and the magic box."

"Connor said his magic didn't work there." She glanced around the room, taking stock of what was there, before looking back at Isaac. "Was all this stuff here?"

Isaac held out his hand and conjured a bottle of water. "No, I conjured it. Our magic works here."

Kate jumped to her knees, adrenaline wiping away her lethargy. "Then we can flash out of here."

"Maybe."

"What do you mean 'maybe'? Why didn't you already flash for help?"

Isaac grasped her hand, and she dropped down, her butt touching her heels. "I couldn't leave you, Kate. If I could have flashed, I didn't know if I'd be able to come back for you. I don't think we're…"

"Where? In Blue Mountain? Or Colorado?" she prompted, needing to know what he thought.

"On Earth."

She wanted to laugh and once more wait for a punch line, but this time she knew Isaac was serious. "What happened when we went through the wall?"

"I'm not sure exactly. You flew backward, and I grabbed onto you. Then it was like we were in the sky, except that it was morning and everything was pitch black. It was windy and freezing cold. Then we fell and landed here in this room. I heard a loud noise, and I think it was the ceiling closing us in."

Kate looked up as if she expected to see the sky. But of course, all she saw was the ceiling, shadows cast across it by the low light emanating from the lanterns.

She scrambled over Isaac and stood on the floor beside the mattress. "Okay, we can flash together."

"No."

"What the hell, Isaac? What do you mean 'no'?"

Isaac finally got off the mattress and stood in front of her, wrapping his hand around the back of her neck again. She loved when he did that, but this wasn't the time to swoon. Nor was it the time to give in. "We need to try to flash," she said as she pulled out of his grasp.

"I know. But you go first."

"Why? Because I'm the female? Like some damsel in distress who is weak and needs to go first?" As soon as the words were out of her mouth, she was repeating her actions from earlier that morning. Isaac wasn't like Ethan, but she held all men at such a distance because of him and her old boyfriends, and she had thought for so long she couldn't trust any man to treat her as an equal.

She expected Isaac would turn away like he had before because she'd insulted him, but he did the unexpected. Closing the distance between them, he once more wrapped his hand around the back of her neck and lowered his forehead to hers. "Yes, because you're female, but—"

"What?" She tried to yank away, but Isaac didn't let go.

"Let me finish, beautiful. Yes, because you're female," he repeated. "But not because you're a damsel in distress. Because you're the only female I've ever cared about. The thought of not being able to get back to you if I got out and you didn't would kill me."

He pulled back and looked down into her eyes, and this time she did swoon. Her knees went weak, but she also felt a panic coming on because of the emotion she saw in his eyes. Caring meant vulnerability, and she had resisted it for so long, she wasn't sure she was ready to let it in.

"That's why we need to flash together," she said again, but it sounded lame even to her after what he'd said.

"I can't do that, Kate." Isaac stepped back. "Please, you flash first, and if you make it out of here, I'll follow you."

As much as she wanted to argue again that she was strong, she sucked it up. Isaac had taken care of her this far; she couldn't hurt him just because she wanted to make a point. Kate nodded, then pulled on her magic and tried to flash.

Nothing happened. "Maybe my magic doesn't work in here like yours."

"Try conjuring something."

Holding out her hand, she conjured a box of condoms.

Isaac looked at the box and barked out a laugh. "Well, it's safe to say your magic works."

Kate tossed the box onto the bed. "But you're not going to try to flash, are you?" she asked quietly.

"No. I can't."

Once more, the urge to argue roared up in her, but this time she ignored it. After everything he said, she couldn't ask him to risk leaving her.

He went back to the bed and sat, leaning against the wall before holding out his hand to her. "Come over here."

She grasped his hand and laughed as he hauled her over his body, where she landed on his other side.

"I think you need to kiss me since you manhandled me like that."

"My pleasure, baby," he whispered before his mouth descended to hers. The kiss was slow and soft, nothing like the one from minutes earlier. Isaac was telling her something with the kiss, but she wasn't sure she was ready to listen yet.

She put her hand on his chest, gently pushing him away. "Lying on this mattress is fine, but I want to sit up as we figure out our next steps." Taking his offered hand, she put her other hand on the wall to reposition herself.

"Oh shit!" She pulled her hand away from the wall as if it had burned her.

"What happened?"

"I felt…" Tentatively, she reached out with her fingers and touched the wall again. "There's malevolence in this wall… or maybe something evil made the wall. I'm not sure which, but it's not good." Scrambling over Isaac, she stumbled to her feet and yanked at him. "You have to get off the mattress! It's not safe to lean against the wall."

Thankfully, he got off the bed without questioning her. "What if we conjured a bedframe with a headboard?" Isaac asked. "There isn't enough space in this room for a comfy living room suite."

She knew he was trying to take the focus off the evil permeating the walls, and once more, she was thankful for his patience and easygoing attitude. In all the time they'd been together, she had just taken it for granted, thinking he went with the flow because he only wanted sex. But that wasn't it at all. Isaac was patient with her and knew how to keep her calm.

Not wanting to dwell on that either, she looked at the mattress. "Should we disappear the mattress and start again?"

"Sounds good."

"What are you waiting for?"

"Nothing. I tried to disappear it, but it didn't work. You try."

Kate focused on the mattress, but like her body when

she tried to flash, it stayed exactly where it was. "Nope." She shook her head. "I guess we can bring things in but can't send things out."

Isaac frowned. "That doesn't make sense, but then, nothing about this room makes sense."

"Oh…" she said as a thought came to her. "We've tried to send ourselves and the mattress out of the room, but they're big. What if we tried something small?"

Isaac's grin seemed bright in the low light. "Like a note?"

"Exactly." Kate conjured a small piece of paper and a pen. "What should we say?"

"Since we don't know where we are, we can't tell them a location…"

His words trailed off, and for the first time since she'd woken up, she sensed a loss of hope in Isaac. Maybe sometimes he did need her to be the strong one. "No problem." She kneeled on the floor with the piece of paper, using the hard surface to write. "We'll just tell them we're alive, in another dimension, and to look for us."

When she was finished, she jumped up and handed him the note. "Why don't you do the honors?"

Isaac took the note, but it remained in his fingers. He handed the note back to her. "You try."

After several attempts, Kate laid the note on the mattress and tried not to let the disappointment settle in too deep. "That's a bust. Let's conjure the bedframe."

Working together, it didn't take them long to conjure a bedframe and box spring and haul the mattress on top. And if Kate purposely conjured a few too many pillows and a flowery blanket that she'd never use at home, that was okay because she got Isaac to laugh.

They stripped down, leaving their clothes in a pile on the floor. After tossing most of the pillows to the end of the bed, they crawled inside and pulled the blankets over them.

Kate snuggled into Isaac and was drifting off to sleep when she felt him shift into a sitting position. "What's wrong?"

"Nothing. I just remembered you had your phone in your back pocket."

She sat up too, as her phone drifted into his palm.

"You don't think we'll be able to call out, do you?"

"No. And you have no reception," he said, turning the phone to face her. "I just thought it might be good to keep track of the time." He conjured a battery block and cord and plugged the phone in.

"You're charging it? Doesn't it need data?"

"No. As long as we keep it charged, the internal battery will keep the calendar and clock working." He passed her the phone. "You'll need to unlock it and turn off any apps running so it won't use as much battery."

Kate took the phone. "One, zero, two, eight," she said as she unlocked her phone. "That's the password, so you'll be able to check the time too. It's the date I bought my land. October twenty-eighth." The purchase had been such a momentous occasion for her that she would never forget the date. It had been a turning point too. Maybe today would be another one. November twenty-fourth. One, one, two, four.

When she finished shutting down all the apps, she passed the phone back to Isaac. "It's the twenty-fourth today."

"I know."

"Thanksgiving is in four days. Do you think we'll make it out of here by then?"

"I hope so, baby."

Isaac put the phone on the floor beside the bed and moved back down under the covers, pulling her with him.

She hoped they'd be home soon too.

Isaac could count on one hand the number of mornings he'd woken up with Kate in his arms, and he'd still have a couple of fingers to spare. Sleepovers meant commitment to Kate, and for the first couple of months of their relationship, he'd been okay with taking things slow. But somewhere along the way, he'd wanted more.

The feeling of waking up beside her this morning, no matter where they were, had felt right to him. He'd been relishing it as she slept tucked into his side.

Since he hadn't bothered to look at Kate's phone, he had no idea how long he'd been awake or what time it was. His guess was he'd been awake about an hour, but time didn't seem to exist in their little room.

He felt her stir a moment before she rolled over to face him. "Good morning, beautiful," he said quietly as he leaned down and kissed her.

"Oh, minty fresh," she said against his lips and then her breath was minty too. "Thank god our magic still works."

"Mmm," he mumbled against her lips as he kissed her.

"Wait." She pushed against his chest as she struggled into a sitting position. "I have to go pee."

In the light from the lanterns, he saw her look around the room. Nothing had changed since the night before, but he guessed she was hoping it had. When she turned back to him, her eyes looked as wide as saucers. "Oh no."

"No problem," he said, pushing back the covers. "Like you said, we've got our magic." He got out of bed and pictured the portable toilet his mom had bought to take camping when he and his brother were younger.

After conjuring the toilet, he set it on the floor against the wall, kitty-corner to the end of the bed. Since the room was so small, it wasn't as if he could put it in a far corner.

"Is that what I think it is?"

Isaac glanced over his shoulder at Kate, but he couldn't see her face clearly in the semi-darkness. It didn't matter; the panic in her voice told him how she felt.

Facing the wall again, mostly to hide his smile, he conjured a double-folding screen, about five feet high and just over two feet wide. They would need to be careful because it wouldn't take a lot to fill up the small space.

Kate rubbed up against his shoulder when she came over to him, and he felt her shiver. The room hadn't gotten any warmer, but right now, he didn't think that was why a frown marred her beautiful features. She peered around the screen at the toilet. "Does that really work?"

"Yes, it even flushes." Pushing aside the screen, he pulled the device forward so they'd have some room. "You need to pump this to create the water pressure first. Then, when you've done your business, you pull this lever…" He demonstrated. "It opens the bottom tank. Then you flush. Everything is sealed in the tank below, even the smell."

Placing the toilet back against the wall, he stood and walked around her, pushing the screen back into place."

"Oh my god," she groaned from behind the screen. "I'm supposed to do *my business*, as you called it, while you're in the room? You'll hear me!"

Isaac smirked and stuck his head around the screen. "Where would you like me to go, Kate?"

Her glare told him she had a few places in mind, then she looked down at the toilet. "I hope they find us soon," she whispered.

In two strides, he was back at the bed and picked up the phone. "I'll play some music, but we'll have to make sure we keep an eye on the battery level and keep it charged. If the battery dies, the clock may not work."

He checked the time on the phone—his own internal clock was useless after such a short time. It was eleven in the morning; they'd been missing for twenty-four hours already.

Not mentioning the time to Kate, he opened the phone's music app to see she had quite a few playlists downloaded. Skimming through the songs, he settled on "I Did Something Bad" by Taylor Swift. That ought to do the trick. Turning up the volume, he pressed play.

After Kate finished, he handed over the baby wipes he'd conjured and then took his turn behind the screen. The music stopped and he smiled, figuring she'd done it on purpose to see if she could rattle him and not to save the battery. Good thing he wasn't shy.

When he used a baby wipe for his hands, he conjured a

garbage bag and put it beside the screen. The room was already filling up. Living in one hundred square feet without a way to dispose of anything was going to be a challenge. "We'll have to be careful deciding what to conjure," he said, joining her on the bed and pulling the blankets up to keep them both warm. "Or we'll quickly run out of places to put things."

Kate sighed and curled up next to him. "I hope we're not here long enough for that to happen."

Isaac feared they might be. Since even he didn't know where they were despite being awake during the entire journey, he figured it would take a while for their friends to figure it out. His even bigger fear was that they wouldn't be able to figure it out at all. And if their friends thought they were dead, then no one would even be looking for them.

Keeping his thoughts to himself, he conjured some fruit. "Banana or grapes?" he asked, holding the fruit out for Kate.

"A bit of both?"

"Sure." After peeling the banana, he handed her half and they each took some grapes.

Once they finished the fruit, he conjured water into the bottles he had created the night before. Without scaring Kate, he'd have to make sure she knew not to create any more waste than necessary. It wasn't that he wanted to coddle her, but he needed her to stay hopeful. Since he had no idea the distance they'd traveled—only that it seemed far—he wasn't as hopeful they'd be found as he wished he could be.

Isaac put their banana peel and grape stems in the garbage bag and frowned when he turned back to the bed.

Kate was kneeling on the mattress with her palms above the headboard, flat against the wall, and with her eyes closed.

"Any change?" he asked as he climbed back onto the bed and settled against the headboard.

"No. It still feels evil."

He pulled Kate between his legs, her back to his chest. Not only did he want to get her away from the wall, he was going to take full advantage of their forced proximity. Isaac wasn't happy they were stuck wherever the hell they were, but… making lemonade, and all that jazz… he was going to enjoy the time he had with Kate.

She relaxed back against him without even a small protest, and something settled within him.

With his arms wrapped around her, he let his hands stay loose in her lap beside hers. Neither of them said anything for several minutes. Isaac guessed Kate was as lost in her thoughts as he was.

Letting his mind wander, he went over everything she had accused him of the day before. Although she was wrong on several fronts and he knew she had been projecting her fear onto him, it had gotten him thinking about trust. Ever since they'd been dumped into this room, the idea of trust had been running through his mind. If he had trusted Kate more, he might have tattooed her over a week ago, and Maverick might already have been a thing of the past.

Isaac remembered what Damon had said about them being sexist. If him considering the strong women he knew as stubborn instead of respecting and trusting their judgment like he would a man's, maybe Damon was right.

He bounced the concepts back and forth in his mind

for a while. Trust and respect were two-way streets, and maybe that was another way Isaac had failed. He had told Damon that Kate was stubborn for not just accepting that he couldn't give her the tattoo. Yet he'd never explained why. Perhaps Isaac hadn't trusted Kate enough to tell her the truth about what had happened.

If he wanted her to be vulnerable with him and open up, then he was going to have to do the same, no matter how much it hurt.

"Kate?"

"Hmm?"

"I should have told you why I refused to tattoo you."

She shifted in his lap, and he spread his legs so she could sit sideways and see him, the blankets falling around her hips.

Looking into her eyes made his guilt harder to confess, but she deserved the truth. "If a person's essence gives me the slightest bit of resistance, I won't tattoo them."

"I know that, but why?"

"Because I tattooed my brother and it led him to commit suicide."

Isaac's internal pain was etched on his face. Kate wished there was something she could do to ease it. When she lifted her hand to his face, he captured it and kissed her palm. Then he gently rotated her hips so she was once more leaning back against him, his arms circling her. She smiled when the blankets floated up around them. Even dealing with his own pain, he thought of her comfort.

He didn't have to voice the words for her to understand that sometimes it was easier to talk when you weren't facing the person you were talking to. She picked up one of his hands in both of hers and trailed one finger along his palm and then each of his fingers.

Isaac's hands were scarred and strong, just like him. She'd watched him work before and admired what he could do, especially the magic tattoos. But not once had she considered that there could be a cost for him.

She continued to trace his fingers and slowly massage his hands but didn't speak. The urge to ask him about his brother was so strong it felt like it had its own pulse within her body, but she refused to heed it.

Isaac had never pushed her to talk, only asked and waited. It was her turn to do the same for him.

"Austin was five years younger than me," Isaac said quietly, finally breaking the silence. "He was only sixteen when our dad died. It felt like the worst thing that could ever happen to us."

Kate didn't say she understood, because this was Isaac's story, but she did understand. More than she wished she did. She'd been a young teenager when her own dad died.

She continued to lazily rub Isaac's hand. After several minutes, she thought Isaac wasn't going to say any more, but then he spoke again.

"When Austin was eighteen, he asked me for a memorial tattoo for our dad. By that time, I'd been tattooing for more than five years professionally, so I thought it would be a piece of cake. But when I put my hands on Austin, my magic rejected the idea of the tattoo. I told Austin I wouldn't do it, but he hounded me for six months until I gave in. A few months later, he was dead because the tattoo drove him crazy."

Kate's specialty was sensing feelings in objects, not people, but in that moment, she swore she could feel Isaac's pain in his hands. Pushing some heat into her own hands, she cupped both of his in hers, letting her warmth seep into him. It wouldn't ease the pain of his loss, but maybe the heat would feel good.

If she had never pushed for him to help her, maybe he wouldn't be reliving his pain right now.

Not only had she projected her pain and insecurities onto Isaac, she'd forced him to deal with something painful in his own past. Now it was her turn.

"I was about ten or so when I saw the Disney movie *Mulan.* My friends all wanted to be like Disney princesses and get the prince, but not me."

She felt Isaac chuckle against her back. "Why am I not surprised?"

His comment made her smile as she remembered. "I was fascinated with the movie, but not because of Mulan herself. Sure, she was a badass, but it was the sword that had me riveted. I wanted to be able to make a sword like that."

She gave a small sardonic laugh, remembering her friends in their princess Halloween costumes and her in her jeans and safety goggles wielding a cardboard sword. "I must have watched that movie a hundred times just to see the swords. I'd always had a bit of artistic talent, but I'd never done more than play around with sketches or do what I had to for art class. Until that year."

Looking at Isaac's hands in hers, she slowly ran one finger along each of his. He took one of her hands in his and linked their fingers. Both of them were artists; they just used different mediums.

Their similarities had drawn her to him as much as they'd scared the crap out of her.

"Drawing swords became my obsession. As soon as I finished my homework, I would grab my sketchbook and design swords. The internet was only just becoming commonplace back then so there wasn't a lot about swords and blacksmithing like there is now. But I got books from the library."

Kate filled up book after book with her sketches. She still had every one of them in a box somewhere.

Isaac rubbed his thumb over hers to let her know he was listening, but he didn't interrupt.

"I think I was about fifteen or so when my dad came into my room to ask me to do something. I don't even know what because he only said, 'Kate, can you—' before he looked at the library books about swords and black-smithing all over my bed. He grinned and said he might have something better."

She laughed as her eyes misted over when she remembered what happened next.

"Dad asked me what kind of swords I was most inter-ested in and what type of designs. I went on and on about Viking broadswords and the different types of Damascus patterns I'd been reading about. Then Dad conjured a sword. The blade was over three feet long and far heavier than I thought it would be. At that point, I'd never actually held a sword before. I was mesmerized." She felt a burning in the backs of her eyes but called up her magic and blinked, drying her eyes.

"Oh god," she giggled. "Mom came into my room to

say it was dinner time, and oh boy, you should have seen the look on her face. Dad was definitely in the proverbial doghouse that night. Mom was so angry that Dad had conjured me a real, deadly weapon, and not only right in my room, but that he let me keep it."

"Do you still have that sword?" Isaac asked softly.

"Yeah, it's in a place of honor in my bedroom, above my dresser." The smile fell from her face when she realized Isaac had never been in her bedroom. She had worked so hard to keep her distance for fear he'd hurt her that she had done them both a disservice by not letting him really know her at all.

Taking a deep breath, she forged ahead. "The day I got accepted for a swordsmith's apprenticeship was the best day of my entire life. I already felt like I knew so much. I had studied everything I could get my hands on to learn about forging and stock removal. Theoretically, I knew about heating, holding, hitting, and shaping. Sure, I knew theory was different than practice, but I was so ready to learn..." She let her voice trail off as several negative experiences from that apprenticeship came to her mind.

"Was it what you thought it would be?"

Isaac's question was so simple, but the answer was more complicated than an intricate Damascus pattern. "I never thought being a woman would hold me back as much as it did. Let's just say it taught me that sometimes skills and dedication don't matter. Men will take whatever they want, whether it's their due or not. They also make decisions without consulting you."

"Woah." Lifting her by her upper arms, Isaac turned her until she was half-facing him. "We're not all like that."

"Really? If the shit at the restaurant the other night

hadn't happened, would you have finally agreed to tattoo me anyway?" Kate slid off the bed so she could stand, giving herself some space and distance from Isaac. She wanted to believe she'd been wrong about Isaac—that he was different—but thinking of her apprenticeship had brought all her old hurts to the surface. Superimposed over them was an image of Isaac standing in her shop refusing to tattoo her.

Isaac moved over so his feet were on the floor while he still sat on the edge of the bed, not crowding her. "I don't know… but it wasn't because I was making decisions for you, Kate. Or because you're a woman. I needed to listen to my magic."

"Because I'm only good enough to fuck? But not to respect?"

Isaac held up his hands as if to ward off an attack. "Kate, don't you dare go there again! I told you yesterday how much I respect you and it wasn't me who wanted the friends-with-benefits thing."

When he finally stood, Kate backed up a step. Not because she was worried he'd hurt her. She wasn't. It was because she needed the space between them. If he pulled her into his arms, she knew she'd crumble.

"I want to date you," he said, his voice much lower now. "I want to make love with you and learn everything there is to know about you!"

"No! No, no, no. You agreed to sex only. Then you went and fucked it up!" she yelled. The emotions she'd been shoving down for months burned so hot that she couldn't hold them in any longer.

Maybe it was everything she'd been through—all the attacks—or just the situation they found themselves in now, but her emotions were begging to be let free. They bubbled up inside her like molten lava in a way that scared her more than death.

"You made me feel things I didn't want to feel ever again! You overtook my thoughts, and it's like you crawled right into my soul! I don't want that!" A sob ripped from her throat, but she forced herself to continue. "It's too powerful! The feeling... it... it gives you the power to shred me!"

Kate ignored the burning behind her eyes and focused on her anger, letting it build to a crescendo. "Fuck you, Isaac! Fuck you for changing the rules! I didn't want to fall in love with you!"

Isaac stood still, watching as Kate's chest heaved, her breaths rapid as she struggled not to cry. He'd been falling for Kate for months, but it was during the last two weeks that he realized he wasn't just falling anymore. He had already fallen, like right over a sharp cliff, and landed hard.

Over the last two weeks, she'd been injured or in a trance three times. Three times he had rushed to her, his heart in his throat, not knowing if she was okay. Three times he had feared he would lose her, either from injury or because that chip on her shoulder would grow so large it would never let him get close.

During those times, he realized his love for her had the ability to shred him too. Their love wasn't roses and candlelight dinners. It wasn't gentle and nice. It was raw and emotional and so fucking powerful that it terrified the shit out of him like nothing else ever had.

If Isaac could choose a less powerful love, a less scary love—one that was sweet and soothing—he wouldn't.

Maybe in the past, before he knew what it was like to love Kate, but not now. Not if it meant passing up the all-consuming intensity he felt for this amazingly strong, stubborn, brave, beautiful woman.

Isaac took a step toward Kate, and she tried to back up, but she hit the folding screen he'd conjured earlier. Reaching out, he steadied the screen, then wrapped his hand around the back of her neck. It had become his go-to move with her. If he let his magic out, he could feel her essence through his palm whenever pulled her close. But he didn't this time, not yet. He left a few inches of space between them as he looked into her eyes. "Tell me again," he said, his voice raspy with emotion.

He was sure she knew what he wanted, but she shook her head, yet she didn't pull away from his grasp.

"Yes. Say it," he demanded.

Kate shook her head again. "No. I don't want to feel it," she choked out.

He caressed her cheek with his thumb, wiping away her tears. "It doesn't matter what you want. We don't get to pick some of our feelings, like love. That's why they're so powerful." Leaning forward, he brushed his lips along hers. Just a feather-light touch. "Tell me, Kate."

Isaac could have gone first and told her how much he loved her. How he'd been falling for her for months. That thoughts of her filled his every waking moment. But he didn't. He needed Kate to face these emotions and for this moment to be her choice. Pulling back just enough to see her eyes, his thumb continued to caress her cheek as he watched her.

"I thought it would just be a few nights of fun sex," she whispered. "Then you decided to stay. I told myself that was good—I'd get regular sex whenever I wanted. I'd be satisfied. I… I thought I could put what we had in a nice little box and keep it locked up tight. But… right from the beginning, you fucking scared me with how much you made me feel."

The more she said, the lower her voice became, as if she was afraid to say the words out loud. But Isaac hung on to each one.

"But then… somewhere along the way, the box cracked open. I…" Her voice was barely audible now. "I fell in love with you, Isaac."

In this dark, cold room, with no way to know if people were searching for them, if they'd ever make it out, Isaac felt like he had suddenly been given the sun, the moon, and all the stars wrapped up in a big, shiny bow.

Not once in the years since his family had fractured with his dad's death and then his brother's had he felt whole like he did in that instant. It didn't matter where they were because Kate loved him. It didn't even matter that she didn't want to love him, because she did.

"Do you love me?" she asked, her voice trembling.

"I do. I love you, Kate."

Isaac bent, and putting one arm under Kate's legs and the other cradling her back, he picked her up and carried her to the bed and laid her down. "I want to strip you slowly and then make love to every inch of your body."

She huffed out a small laugh. "But we'll freeze."

He chuckled. "Yup, that's what I was thinking. We'll have to compromise." Using his magic he removed their clothing, leaving it folded on the floor. Then he quickly climbed into the bed beside her and pulled up all the blankets.

When she shivered, he sent his magic throughout his body, as well as into his hands, warming her skin wherever it touched his.

"Ahhh, warmth."

Moving up onto his side, he shifted so he was hovering over her. "I love you, Kate." Not waiting for a response, he lowered his lips to hers. He wanted to keep the pace slow and make love to her, letting her feel his love.

He kept the kiss slow, gliding his lips over hers, his tongue playing with hers, for as long as he could. Smiling to himself, he knew it wouldn't last. Not that he was complaining. He loved how passionate Kate was, and he could show her he loved her in a hard and fast way too.

"Please, Isaac, no teasing. I don't want slow."

He kissed down her jaw, dragging it out for a few more seconds. "You never want slow," he said, smiling at her in the dim light.

"That's because slow is overrated. Make love to me, Isaac. Please," she tacked on when she nipped at his lip.

"Are you warm?" he asked.

"Yes. Why?"

Instead of answering, he flipped their positions so she was now straddling him.

She laughed and rubbed herself back and forth over him, her pussy already wet, lubricating his cock. When he handed her a condom, she took her time easing it down his length and then stroked him. Her fingers were just loose enough to tease.

Reaching up with both hands, he played with her nipples until she was writhing on him, and he knew he wouldn't last much longer. He pulled her down, took one of her nipples in his mouth, and bit down just shy of causing real pain.

Her groan spurred him on, and he continued sucking her nipples. Reaching behind her, he kneaded her ass, and she groaned, rocking against him faster. He loved her ass, and it was one of her erogenous zones—it would drive her to the peak in no time at all.

"Fuck, yes," she screamed as she rocked back and forth on the length of his cock, rubbing along it, creating a delicious friction.

"Now, Isaac. I need you."

Releasing her nipple with a soft pop, he brought his hands forward and reached one between them, guiding himself to her hot, wet sex.

Kate braced herself on his shoulders and lifted up. Then she slowly lowered herself over him, sliding down until he was fully seated in her tight pussy. He was so hard for her that he was almost ready to come without either of them moving. But why deny them both the pleasure?

Wrapping his hands around her hips, he helped her move up and down on his cock, keeping her pace slow to prevent her from taking them both over the edge too quickly.

He let the pressure build for several long minutes.

"Please, Isaac. More. I'm so close."

As much as he wanted to drag out their pleasure even longer, he was close too and barely hanging on.

Letting go of her hips, he reached between her legs and rubbed her clit. Her breathing picked up, and as he felt her start to tighten around him, he rubbed faster and drove his hips up.

"Fuuuuck. Isaac!"

He loved hearing her scream his name as she tightened around him and then ignited from the pleasure she took from him.

Taking her hips in both of his hands again, he lifted his own hips higher and tilted his pelvis, changing the angle as he drove into her again and again.

Isaac felt another orgasm rip through Kate, and it was his undoing, pulling him over the edge with her.

When she collapsed on top of him, they were both breathing like they'd just sprinted a hundred-yard dash.

Making quick work of the condom and cleaning them both up, Isaac tucked Kate back into his side. Then he pulled the blankets up, wrapping them around them both.

"I love you, Kate," he whispered against her hair. Now that he'd said it, he wanted to say it all the time so she always knew.

"I love you, too." She ran her fingers along his chest, tracing his tattoo, as he'd seen her do in the past. He hadn't turned the lanterns off yet, and he loved watching her fingers on his skin. "Why the owl?"

He was sure his love for her grew in that moment. It was the first time she had ever asked about his tattoos. She'd shown her appreciation for them and his body, but not once had she asked about the meaning behind them. It was one more thing she had done to keep her distance.

Laying his hand over hers, he held it over one of the owl's wings, right over his own heart. "Owls represent the ability to see beyond the surface and uncover hidden truths. My dad had a tattoo just like this. He said it was to always remind him what a special gift his magic was because he could feel emotions in people that others couldn't. It was a gift he would never take lightly."

His dad said those exact words to him when they realized that Isaac had inherited his dad's special gift. A few months later, his dad inked the owl on him.

"It's beautiful," she said, and he felt her yawn against him.

"Get some sleep, beautiful."

When he heard her breathing even out, he let sleep overtake him as well. His last thought before he succumbed was that Kate was his biggest gift of all, and since they were trapped here, he would never get to enjoy the gift of her for a lifetime.

"Do you think they're looking for us?" Kate asked quietly as she snuggled up against Isaac.

During the first three days in the room, she'd been positive someone would find them. A few times, she had even wondered if their rescuers would interrupt them making love.

If she blocked out everything but being with Isaac, she could even think of this little adventure as a mini vacation. Not a luxury one, but an escape from everyday life.

Besides some of the inconveniences like the toilet and not being able to shower, Kate enjoyed the time with Isaac. They had made love so many times she'd lost count.

Being with Isaac wasn't just about sex anymore. And looking back to the time after the first month or so they were together, it probably never was. Kate knew now she'd been in denial.

Just like she'd been in denial when she refused to admit Isaac had been making love to her for a long time.

Especially after they both agreed to get tested for sexually transmitted diseases, even though she was on the pill, because they'd wanted skin-to-skin contact.

She wished they could have that same intimate contact now, but she'd always refused to conjure birth control pills—it was a risk she wasn't willing to take. The only good thing about condoms now was that they were less messy.

Kate had never been a prude or a prissy princess, but being in one room with someone twenty-four seven with no running water and limited space was not for the faint of heart.

When they weren't making love, they were in the bed anyway. Not like they had any room to conjure more furniture, but mostly it was to keep warm. The room seemed to hover just below a comfortable temperature.

This morning, her hope started to fade as they welcomed their fourth day in the room. If it wasn't for her phone, it would have felt like one very long day. Time had no meaning.

When Kate realized it had been several minutes and Isaac hadn't answered her question, she lifted onto her elbow so she could see his eyes. He was lying on his back, one arm wrapped around her.

"Isaac? Did you hear me?"

He let out a long sigh. "I heard you... I was just thinking about how to answer. I want to say yes, I think they're looking for us, but I don't know."

"You don't think Sam and Ben saw us get pulled through the wall?"

Isaac reached over and pulled her back down into his side, then floated the blankets up around them. She hadn't realized she was cold until she felt the warmth of his skin against her.

"Again… I don't know. Sam and Ben were facing Maverick, and although I hope they saw us get sucked into the hole, I…"

A couple of weeks ago, Kate would have jumped on Isaac to continue, wanting to know why he paused. But she was learning that sometimes he needed time to formulate his answers. They'd been together for months, and she was only just learning those little things about him.

Rolling over so he faced her, Isaac used one hand to push her hair back from her face and then gently ran his fingers over her cheek. If he'd done that in the past, she hadn't noticed, but now she was coming to crave the gesture, needing his touch.

"I just keep wondering…" Isaac continued. "Maybe they saw us go through the wall or maybe Maverick made it seem like we died."

"Why would he do that?"

"Again… I don't know. But he said he was going to kill you with a twist… If he wanted to only make it seem like you died, keeping you here could be the twist. Or making you suffer could be the twist. I don't think he expected me. I just came along for the ride." One corner of his lip arched in a small smirk.

"I'm glad you did." Her voice choked on the last word as she envisioned what could have happened if Isaac hadn't been here. She may never have made it into the room safely, and even if she had, she might have gone stir-crazy.

Isaac closed the few inches between them and kissed

her. It was a leisurely kiss, something she hadn't allowed before. She had been so intent on keeping things impersonal that she had missed out on so much with him. And not just intimacy but getting to know him as well.

Many people probably considered sex to be the most intimate of acts between two people, but Kate had learned the hard way that it wasn't always. When she had been with Ethan, the sex had been good—not great like with Isaac—but she didn't know that then. She had given Ethan her body, and in turn, her trust and respect. When he'd thrown all that back in her face, she had learned that sex was just a physical act. It was the feelings that made it so much more.

And it was all those pesky feelings she'd tried so hard to avoid having with Isaac. He'd been right… they didn't get to pick some feelings, like love. But with trust, she had a choice. She could choose to trust Isaac. By telling him things she'd never told anyone, she would start to build that trust.

She opened her eyes, not even knowing when she had closed them, and looked into Isaac's beautiful light gray ones. He was still stroking her face and her hair, giving her his warmth.

Taking his hand from her face so she could hold it, she rolled onto her back. He left his hand in hers, and like before, she gently stroked his fingers and palm. Something about holding his hand was soothing. It gave her a connection to him, as she knew she wouldn't get through this if she was looking into his eyes. She didn't expect she'd see judgment there—Isaac wasn't like that—but she didn't want to show him her shame either.

"When you asked me the other day if my apprenticeship was what I thought it would be... and I said I never thought being a woman would hold me back. That skills and dedication didn't matter... that men take whatever they want... I'm so sorry I projected that on to you, Isaac." She choked out the last words, feeling the weight of all that she'd put onto him because of her shame.

Isaac shifted up onto his elbow so he was looking into her eyes. "Hey, beautiful. It's okay. We've been over that." He lifted his hand from hers and stroked her hair back before he kissed her softly. "I forgive you," he whispered.

She gave him what was probably a weak smile, but it must have been enough since he laid back down and put his hand back into hers.

"The blacksmith shop I was apprenticing in was Henry's. Jack mentioned him the other night. Anyway, he's an amazing man. He took me under his wing and taught me so much."

She absently played with Isaac's fingers as she thought about how nervous she'd been when Henry had first taught her how to use a forge. Just the heat from the fire was scary enough, let alone everything she had to learn.

"There were three other apprentices there—all men— and they believed a woman had no place being a sword-smith." She snorted softly at the huge understatement. "I tried not to let their comments bother me, and I went every day to learn. But their derision and the tension it created was a constant stressor that was slowly eating away at my confidence. Some days it didn't seem to matter how much I was improving, or the praise Henry gave me, because the snide and sexist comments were a continuous mindfuck."

Isaac turned his hand over in hers and gave her fingers

a gentle squeeze. His silent support gave her enough strength to continue.

"When I was in my fourth year at Henry's and was about to receive my certificate of mastery, he hired a new swordsmith. Only one of the original three guys was still there. One had quit and the other had finished his apprenticeship and took a job elsewhere.

"I remember going into work one day and being totally relieved after hearing that one of the three sexist assholes had quit. Even though there were two left, my life got a little bit easier… Anyway… The new guy was Ethan. He had studied under someone else, but Henry had seen some of his work and had been impressed. We had a lot of work, and Henry needed to bring on someone new, so he was going to take a chance on Ethan."

Isaac never said a word, but every so often, she felt the heat he pushed into his fingers, giving her his warmth. They had the blankets pulled up around them, but their hands were exposed to the chilly air.

"Even though Henry is magic, it isn't a requirement to work for him. Two out of the three condescending idiots were non-magic. The one that remained was magic, but I think that was just a coincidence. Ethan was magic too, and the first time I saw him, I was leery, considering everything I'd been through."

Kate didn't mention how attracted she'd been to Ethan, even while she was distrusting. Ethan wasn't overly tall, but his shoulders were broad, and he carried himself with an air of confidence that she admired.

"He was charming and didn't seem to have a problem with a woman in the trade. I was cautious around him at first, always waiting for a derogatory comment, but he wasn't like that. And once I graduated from my apprenticeship, Henry offered me a full-time position, and Ethan and I began working on projects together.

"One night, after Henry and the others had left, Ethan asked me out for coffee. Normally, I would have gone home to shower, but with us both being magic, I didn't have to worry about using it around him. Once we were cleaned and changed, we went for coffee, and that turned into a late-night dinner and then drinks."

Ethan had been so easy to talk to, and having someone who loved swordsmithing like she did and who was magic? It was like a match made in heaven.

"It wasn't long before we were dating and then sleeping together. I was so in love with him..." She let her voice trail off as she remembered how Ethan had made her feel, the attention he'd given her and what she'd thought was respect after being treated like an inferior for so long. She'd eaten that shit right up.

"We'd only been together for two months when he proposed. He was everything I thought I wanted and needed..." Isaac rubbed his thumb over her hand, and she knew he was letting her know she could tell him anything.

"Shortly after we were engaged, a client Henry had worked with before came to him with a really big project. He wanted a custom sword to display in his office, and money was no object. The kind of sword he was asking for could take months to make."

Kate felt her palms begin to sweat, even in the cool temperature of the room. Thinking back to Ethan's betrayal and the embarrassment and shame he caused ratcheted up her anxiety every time. It didn't matter how much time had passed.

Like before, Isaac's thumb rubbed her hand, and then he turned her palm over and ran his finger along it. Such a simple gesture, but she got it. He wasn't going to judge.

She wasn't sure she could go into the details. Nor that they mattered. The outcome was what she needed to tell Isaac. The CliffsNotes version was going to have to do. "Henry asked both me and Ethan to come up with some designs to present to the client. I was so excited. I had three final designs that I had worked on tirelessly and was so proud of.

"When the day came to present to the client, Henry, Ethan, and I went to the client's office. Ethan said he was nervous and asked me if he could go first. I had seen his designs, and although they were nice, they weren't anything to write home about, so I said sure. Getting his presentation out of the way first was probably a good idea."

Kate expected Isaac had already figured out where this story was going, but she needed to tell him the rest.

"When Ethan opened his portfolio, it was my designs he handed to the client. Henry looked at me; he knew Ethan had stolen them because I had shown them to Henry, but he didn't say anything in front of the client. Henry's reputation was being represented just as much as mine and Ethan's. Anyway... the client loved the designs, and when he asked to see mine, I opened my portfolio to see Ethan's designs were there instead. There was nothing I could do but present them. The client was visibly underwhelmed, but he was at least professional enough not to say anything."

To this day, the embarrassment of that moment felt like acid churning in her gut. "When we got back to the shop, I was sure Henry would tell me I could create the sword since they were my designs. But before he could, Ethan gave Henry his resignation. Said he was going to work at another shop and would be making the sword there. Then..." Kate took a big breath and let it out slowly. "Ethan said now that his career was set, he didn't need me anymore and asked for his engagement ring back."

Kate felt a burning behind her eyes, the stupid telltale sign of tears, but she was tired of crying because of that asshole. She blinked and turned her head so she could look into Isaac's eyes. He had said she was a coward for running away from her feelings, and she needed to prove to him she could face them. Even if she had to face his pity as well.

But it wasn't pity she saw.

"Come here," he said as he lifted his hand out of hers and wrapped it around the back of her neck, pulling her closer. He kissed her then, but it wasn't sweet and soft. His kiss was like a forge's flame, hot and intense, and she willingly submitted, malleable in his hands.

When they pulled back, her heart was racing, but it wasn't from anxiety. They didn't resume their former positions, just stayed as they were, looking at each other, but she reached for his hand and linked her fingers with his.

There was one thing left to tell him. "I thought Ethan stealing my designs and telling me how he had used me was the worst thing that could ever happen to me. But I think maybe Ethan was worried I'd tell people what he'd done. After all, our trade isn't super big. It's a small community and mostly male, so all Ethan had to do was tell a few people I had tried to pass off his designs as my own. He spread the word that as a woman, I just couldn't cut it in the trade.

"It wasn't until a year later that the client Ethan was creating the sword for came back to Henry, disgusted with Ethan's work and pissed because Henry had recommended him. I'm not sure what Henry said to the client, but he gave me a chance and I created the sword from my original design—it was beautiful." She couldn't help but smile when she thought about the sword.

"My reputation was shot among other swordsmiths, but when I went out on my own, with Henry's blessing, that client helped spread the word about the quality of my work. It took time, but now my business is thriving."

"I always wondered where that chip on your shoulder came from," Isaac teased as he closed the gap between them and nipped at her lower lip.

Kate realized that she could take the teasing from Isaac and didn't feel like she needed to defend herself. "Ha-ha, funny man," she said as she pushed up into a sitting position. "I'm hungry. What time is it?"

Isaac leaned over the bed and glanced at the phone on the floor. "I guess we missed dinner. It's already seven."

"What do you—" Before she could even ask what Isaac felt like having, he had retrieved the two plates they conjured a couple of days ago and placed huge sandwiches on them, passing one to her.

In one of their many conjuring sessions, they decided to reuse as many items as they could, like plates and water bottles, since they couldn't make anything disappear.

Death by falling stacks of plates and cups was not her preferred way to go.

"Thank you. It looks delicious. Turkey?"

"Yes. Happy Thanksgiving, baby," he said softly as he bent toward her and kissed her briefly before going back to his sandwich.

Kate had forgotten it was Thanksgiving. She sent a wish out into the universe that this would be the only holiday they would spend in the room.

"I THINK we're going to need to conjure more condoms," Kate with a grin, still straddling his legs. Her skin was flushed and she looked happy.

He copied her contagious grin. "I'll get right on that." Then he did, tossing her the new box he conjured.

Funny that sometimes all it took to be happy was a turkey sandwich and some good, hard sex. Isaac wished he could see Kate happy all the time. If they ever got out of this room, he would make her happiness his life's mission.

Sated from both food and sex and as clean as they could get, they were back to leaning against the headboard with the blankets pulled up into their laps.

Isaac heard Kate yawn and turned to her. "You ready to sleep?"

"No, I'm good. I think all the lying around just makes me feel tired. You know… that expending energy creates energy thing. Good thing we were a little active," she teased.

He gave her shoulder a light shove with his. "Good thing. We'll have to keep it up. So you don't get tired and all."

She laughed. "I'll hold you to it."

Because the lack of space in the room was a constant worry, they hadn't created any more lanterns. But on the third day, Isaac had conjured a narrow nightstand, just big enough to hold the phone and charger and one of the lanterns.

It gave him enough light for what he had in mind. Thinking about what supplies he'd need for his idea, he decided against conjuring anything else that would need charging.

A sketchpad with a wood backing and a pencil appeared in his lap, then he conjured both items again. Since he was going to draw, he figured Kate might like to as well. He'd never seen any of her designs, but he had seen some of her work and knew what a talented artist she was.

"Oooh. We're going to draw?" She clapped like a little girl and took one of the pads and a pencil.

"I thought I would draw your tattoo."

Her mouth dropped open, her beautiful brown eyes round with surprise. "Really? You're going to tattoo me when we get out of here?"

"Actually… I thought I could tattoo you while we're here. I envision most of the design being in shades of black and gray, so it will be easy to conjure the ink."

"What about your machine?"

He bumped her shoulder again. "No faith in me?" he said playfully but didn't wait for an answer. "It isn't a complicated machine, and I've conjured one before. I conjure the needles too." He shrugged. "Easier than dealing with suppliers, and I know what I'm getting."

Kate rested her sketchpad in her lap and absently ran her fingers over it. He'd noticed she did that when she wanted to say something but wasn't sure how.

"Are you wondering why now?"

"Yeah. What changed your mind? Besides… needing to do it because of what happened. It's not like that's affecting us in here."

"It doesn't mean you won't need the protection when we get out of here. You'll still need to work with the sword, and my tattoo will help you do that." The magic he would embed in the design would also help protect her when they escaped. Isaac had no idea what they might have to face during their escape or what could be waiting for them, and he'd do anything to keep Kate safe. He hoped down to the bottom of his soul that his words would come true and they would get out of the room.

"But to answer your question… I need to trust that you know what you can handle. I was wrong before for not telling you why I didn't want to do the tattoo. And someone told me that thinking you were stubborn and that you should just trust me was me being sexist."

"Oh my god! Who called you sexist?"

Isaac grinned so big his face almost hurt. He couldn't wait to see Kate's reaction to his answer. "Your brother."

"Holy shit! Damon? My overprotective, controlling, alpha-male brother?"

Her reaction didn't disappoint, and he couldn't help the laugh that escaped him. "You have more than one brother?"

"Uh, no. I'm just surprised."

"He's right, you know," Isaac said before bending his knees and propping the sketchpad on his thighs. "I've always known you were strong, but I thought you were stubborn—"

Kate snorted softly. "I am stubborn."

"Maybe. Or maybe you just know your own mind. That's what Damon was getting at. As long as you can bend when you need to or see compromise if it's possible, that's not being stubborn. It's standing by your principles and going for your dreams."

Isaac picked up his pencil and began recreating the image he'd dreamed about. "Or like I said, if I had explained my reasoning for not wanting to do the tattoo, we could have come to a compromise."

"Is that what you're doing now?"

"I'd like to think so." He met her gaze. "I'll do the tattoo, but we'll take it slow, doing a section a day. If I sense anything is off, we'll stop. And if you sense something's not right, you tell me. Agreed?"

"Agreed."

They were both quiet for a long while as they worked on their sketches. He was almost finished with his and looked forward to inking it on her. Since they didn't have access to a photocopier to transfer the design onto stencil paper, they'd have to get creative, but Isaac had done that before. And magic would come in handy for that.

"Isaac?"

"Hmm?"

"When you were at my shop and you got the warning that you couldn't do the tattoo… what did you feel?"

Looking back on it now, he thought he had interpreted it incorrectly. "The sensation was strong. Stronger than I've ever felt from someone before. It's hard to explain, but it was like something in you was pushing back against something in me."

"You think it was telling you not to tattoo me?"

A part of Isaac wanted to say yes. But it wasn't the whole truth, and if they were ever going to build a deep trust between them, he had to be completely honest with her. "At first, it was such a strange feeling that I thought that must be it. That my magic was saying the tattoo wasn't a good idea. But I was wrong."

"How so?"

He laid his sketchpad and pen on the bed and turned toward her, cupping her neck in the way they'd both come to crave. "I think it was my love for you talking. And the pushback I felt was your love answering. It wasn't warning me—it was trying to make me understand."

15

Kate loved watching Isaac work. She'd seen him work on numerous clients in his shop, chatting them up as they got inked. Yet this was different, because not only was she watching the tattoo take shape, but she could also feel it.

Isaac constantly assessed her, making sure she was okay. Every few minutes, he would stop working and lay his full hand on her, above or to the side of his work. She could feel the heat from his palm soak into her skin, as well as something else, like her magic stirring. The first few times he did it, she wasn't sure what was happening. Then she finally asked him.

It was her love answering his, he said. His magic, how he could feel emotions in people, made it possible. At least, that was his theory. Now she waited for the sensation every time he laid his palm on her.

"Oh my god!"

"What?" Isaac stopped working immediately and looked up.

"Put your hand around my neck like you usually do."

Laying his machine on the bed, Isaac pushed out of his crouched position on the floor and sat next to her as he pulled off his gloves. Kate had worried about the gloves being more waste in the room since Isaac would need many pairs. But, in the end, safety won out, and they chalked up the gloves as being a necessary evil, like condoms.

As soon as he cupped her neck, she closed her eyes. "Do you feel it?" she whispered.

"My magic? Yes. I think it's one of the reasons I love putting my hand on your neck; I can feel your life's essence."

"Not just that," she said quietly, not wanting to intrude too harshly on the moment. "Can you feel my love reaching back to you?"

"I can." His thumb rubbed her cheek, and then she felt his lips softly touching hers and she opened her eyes.

"I hadn't connected the dots until just now. I love you, Isaac."

"And I love you, Turquoise."

She laughed at the name. "Turquoise? You usually call me beautiful or baby. Are you adding to your collection?"

"No, I'm replacing the rest. They're all too generic." He stood and stretched out his back.

"Are you okay?" Since they didn't want to conjure a stool or a tattoo chair, they were making do with the bed and Isaac sitting on it or kneeling on the floor. It wasn't easy on his body, and she worried about him.

She smiled as she remembered how she'd helped him limber up the night before, and she would gladly help him again tonight.

It was day six in the room and the second day of working on her tattoo. Determined to only work on a portion of the design each day, Isaac was taking his time and monitoring her reactions. He was, after all, embedding his magic into Kate's skin. She liked the thought of that.

When he was kneeling on the floor once more, she got back into her reclined position. The design consisted of swirls and paisleys that started on the top of her foot and wound up her calf, stopping at the back of her knee. He had considered going up to her hip, like he'd originally envisioned, but because the tattoo had a magical purpose, the addition of the piece on her arm and shoulder would work better.

Isaac had explained how the design had come to him in a dream and what it meant. After he finished on her left leg, he would put the same design on her right upper arm and shoulder, drifting it up onto the back of her neck. The completed design would protect her entire body.

After Isaac settled back into working, she picked up their previous conversation. "Explain the turquoise thing to me."

He chuckled and glanced at her briefly. "When I knew your design would be shades of black and gray with only one color woven throughout, I had to choose which color I'd use. No… that's not really true. I didn't have to choose because I knew immediately that it would be turquoise. The turquoise stone is rare and valuable." He looked up at her again and winked. "Like you."

"Ahhh, you sweet talker, you," she teased, but she was melting inside. Now that she wasn't constantly trying to keep him away, she was getting to see his romantic side.

Something she didn't even know she would really like because of all those pesky relationship feelings she had tried to ignore for so long. As it turned out, she was beginning to crave them.

"The turquoise color signifies wisdom, tranquility, protection, good fortune, and loyalty. Add beautiful to that list, inside and out, and it represents you perfectly."

"I love it."

When Isaac decided it was time to stop for the day, Kate didn't protest. Her calf was almost finished, and while she couldn't wait to see him add the turquoise, Isaac's peace of mind was more important than her seeing a finished tattoo in the next couple of hours.

By the time Isaac had cleaned up, healed her skin, and they had eaten dinner, Kate felt like she'd been through the wringer. She enjoyed her time with Isaac, but she kept waiting for one of two things: someone to come and rescue them or for the other shoe to drop. As much as she was trying to stay positive, she worried that Maverick had something more in store for them. With so much time to think in a day and so much that was unknown, it was difficult to never think about the worst that could happen. She had decided that she would acknowledge the thought and then shove it aside as best she could.

Curling up with Isaac and talking about random things was the highlight of her day. Sometimes they talked about their childhoods or their favorite this or that. Kate could only hope they'd be rescued soon, and when they were, that she wouldn't lose this with Isaac.

"Will you tell me what happened to Austin?" she asked quietly as they lay skin to skin, her fingers trailing over the tattoo on Isaac's chest.

"I told you he was five years younger than me and sixteen when our dad died, right?"

She nodded against his shoulder.

"After Dad died, Austin asked me to give him a memorial tattoo for our dad. He wanted a large lion and a cub. I drew up the design first, without even checking him with my magic to see if it would work on him."

Isaac chuckled, but it sounded more sad than happy. "After he saw the design, he was even more excited than he'd been before, and that was saying something. Austin was quite the artist, but he didn't have the same magical ability as me and our dad… Now that I think about it, I'm not sure if Austin even had a magic specialty. Not that it matters now."

Isaac's voice trailed off again, and Kate kept up her gentle caress over his chest, waiting for him to continue.

"When I finally checked Austin's compatibility for a memorial tattoo and my magic rejected the idea, Austin was devastated. He accused me of lying, saying I just didn't want to give him the tattoo. I told him that wasn't true and that I'd love to do it. I wouldn't change the design at all, I just wouldn't imbue it with magical properties. And because of that, he could have it anywhere he wanted. He'd always talked about having a big tattoo on his back, but memorial tattoos are usually on the front of the body so the person can place their hand on them. Austin said it wasn't the same and stormed out of the shop."

Isaac picked up her hand from his chest and kissed the back of it before linking their fingers together. "I knew Austin wasn't going to let it drop. He was a tenacious little bugger, and he was going to hound me. I just hadn't realized how much. After six months, he had laid on the guilt so thick that I was swimming in it. I finally broke down and gave him the tattoo. And when I did, Austin asked me to choose the memory to embed in the design. It was easy for me to pick one because I have so many great memories of our dad, and I chose one of the many of him laughing.

"Austin chose to have me tattoo the lion and cub on his chest for easy reach. When he laid his hand on the tattoo, he'd be able to feel our dad's laughter like it was a warm blanket surrounding him."

Maybe one day she would ask Isaac to give her a small memorial tattoo for her dad. She'd thought of it before but hadn't followed through because of that stupid distance thing. She'd have Isaac put it in the same spot on her wrist as the tattoos the Williams women and Isabella had, but unlike their compasses, she'd get a sword.

Isaac rubbed his thumb on hers where their hands were linked, and she knew he was preparing what he'd say next.

"My dad wasn't one of those bigger-than-life kind of guys who can walk into a room and take it over," Isaac said, picking up his story. His voice sounded raspier than it had before.

"Physically, he was tall, like me, only broader, but he was quiet. He didn't have a problem talking to his clients when he needed to and he wasn't a pushover. When Dad said something, people listened. He loved his work, and his staff adored him. But the most important thing to him was his family." Isaac chuckled. "My mom was always going on about how our dad spoiled us. He was strict about some things, like being respectful and getting good grades, but things like bedtime, allotted time on video games, and eating junk food? Dad didn't care. He always said seeing us happy was more important than any of those things."

Kate shivered, noticing the cold in the room as she grew tired. Isaac pulled her in closer with the arm that was wrapped around her and used his magic to warm her up. Yawning as she relaxed into his heat, she was determined to stay awake to hear the rest of his story.

"Dad was only forty-eight when he died of a heart attack. Austin and I were with him at the shop when it happened. It hit us both equally hard, but I think Austin thought the memorial tattoo would help him cope with his grief. When I looked back on things years later, I could see that Austin had been a little too spoiled, and once he got something in his mind, he wasn't willing to give it up, just like the tattoo. I gave him the tattoo in one sitting, and everything seemed fine at first. When I embedded the memory into the tattoo, I felt a bit of pushback from his magic, but nothing crazy..."

Isaac took a deep breath and unlinked his fingers from hers. He ran his lips over the back of her hand and then just held it against his chest, right over the owl's left wing.

"About a month after I gave Austin the tattoo, he quit college. Said he just wasn't feeling it and he'd go back the following semester. I didn't see him more than every couple of weeks because I had my own place and he was still living with our mom. The next time I saw him after he quit school, he looked tired. There were bags under his eyes, and he'd lost weight. He was a pretty lanky guy to begin with, so the weight loss was pretty obvious. He was moody, and my mom said there were days he wouldn't even come out of his bedroom."

Kate wished there was something she could say to diminish some of Isaac's pain. But even magic couldn't take away emotional pain. She knew what was coming and wanted to get him to spit it out, though at the same time, she wanted to prevent him from going any further. Sometimes talking about tragedy helped, and sometimes it made it feel fresh again, and she wasn't sure what would happen for him.

"I began stopping by the house several times a week just to check on him, but I hadn't seen him in two days when my mom phoned the shop in a panic. I flashed to a room in the back of the house just as EMTs were coming in the front door. Austin was already gone by the time my mom found him. He had OD'd.

"Later that night, still in shock, my mom showed me the note Austin had left. It was only a few lines written on a piece of lined paper, saying that Dad's laughter had told him to kill himself so they could be together. Mom started grilling me about the tattoo. She had seen it, but Austin never told her it was a memorial tattoo. My mom crumbled right in front of my eyes. Tears streamed down her cheeks and sobs racked her entire body in a way that I'll never forget."

Isaac paused, and his eyes were glassy when he tilted his head to look at Kate. "I thought she was finally realizing what had happened, but she was blaming herself. She confessed that when I was four, she was miserable. Dad doted on me, and he had his work, but she was unhappy in her job and she said that Dad just brushed it off, not taking her feelings seriously enough. She had an affair and got pregnant with Austin. Since Austin looked a lot like my mom, she never told Dad the truth. I think Dad's laughter in the tattoo slowly drove Austin into a deep depression and maybe the magic even told Austin the truth about who his dad was. I'll never know."

Kate ached for him, but there wasn't a damn thing she could do. Using her magic, she dried her tears, not wanting Isaac to see them since this wasn't about her. She crawled on top of him, lining her body up with his so they were touching from knees to chest. She laid her head on his shoulder, and he pulled the blankets up around them both, wrapping his arms around her.

She didn't say anything, just hoped he could feel her love for him through her skin.

"Go Fish." Isaac watched the grin spread across Kate's face. She only had one card in her hand and there was only one left to pick from.

When she matched the cards, she threw the pair on the bed. "I win. I win. I win," she said, making the bed bounce.

"Again," he groaned. He wouldn't throw a game, even Go Fish, so she could win—she'd hate it—but he enjoyed watching her when she did win.

Playing cards helped pass the time. They'd started out with poker and conjured pennies to use as chips, figuring they were tiny and would fit under the bed. For a change of pace, they'd switched to Gin Rummy and then Go Fish.

They'd been in the room for eight days, and it was becoming harder not to worry. Neither of them brought it up often, as if by silent agreement they had decided not to talk about their worry. Sometimes Isaac would catch Kate with a frown on her face and lost in thought, but she always said it was nothing, and he said the same to her, trying to play off his worry.

There had been times when they'd had no choice but to conjure a few more things. The room had been small from the get-go and now it was crowded, but they tried to keep things as tidy as possible. Deciding to sacrifice more room on the floor, they had conjured a shelving unit to take advantage of some vertical space.

It hadn't taken long for the garbage to start to stink, so they'd conjured a compost bin—the type for indoors with a lid that sealed shut. It didn't perfectly keep the smells at bay, but it was better than before. They'd needed to conjure another portable toilet too. With the bed, the nightstand, the shelving unit, the compost bin, a garbage can, and the screen with the portable toilets, there was almost no floor space left, but the shelves had helped.

The only saving grace was that they could use their magic to clean their clothes, the sheets, and cooking utensils. They could magically clean their bodies as well, but it wasn't as good as the fresh feeling of using soap and water. But even limiting what they could conjure, they were thankful for their magic. Isaac had used his to heal Kate's tattoo.

He had finished her tattoo two days ago and it looked amazing. She had been beautiful before, but now he couldn't take his eyes off her when she was naked. Unfortunately, that was only when they were both huddled under the covers for warmth.

With his design gracing her delicate skin, he would

find himself tracing the pattern on her upper arm and shoulder when they were in bed. And when he wrapped his hand around the back of her neck, he could feel their magic combine. The pops of turquoise in the tattoo were his favorite, and he decided the new nickname was going to stick, but so far, he'd only used it when they made love.

"Another game or do you want to sketch?" Kate asked, breaking into his thoughts.

"Let's sketch. I just want to fill up our water bottles first. You thirsty?"

"No, I'm good."

Isaac tried to read the expression on Kate's face to see if she was telling the truth. "Kate, you need to drink. You can't get dehydrated because you don't want to use the toilet." As soon as the words left his mouth, he knew he sounded like a parent scolding a toddler, but he didn't care. She had to take care of herself because not only did he want her to be healthy, he couldn't imagine adding a health issue to their situation when they couldn't get medical attention.

She laughed at him. "That's not the issue, believe me. I think I got over that embarrassment by day two. I'm just not doing what I normally do in a day, and I haven't been as thirsty. Plus, I never drink as much when I'm cold."

Isaac couldn't fault her logic as he knew he hadn't been drinking as much as he normally did either. But he'd already been worried about how little Kate had been eating. When he'd questioned her, she said she hadn't been hungry because she didn't do anything except sit in a bed all day.

Making a promise to himself that he'd keep an eye on

her food and water intake, he collected the four water bottles they used so he could refill them.

Holding two in his hands, he called on his magic, but something wasn't right. He could feel his magic stir within him, but it wasn't responding like it should. Shaking off the feeling, he focused on refilling the bottles. Nothing happened.

A panic started deep in his gut as he stared at the bottles. Focusing on just one bottle, he tried again. The bottle filled to the top, and he heaved a sigh of relief.

"What's wrong?" Kate asked.

"My magic felt weird for a minute, and I couldn't fill the bottles. But it's fine now."

Isaac closed the lid on the first bottle and concentrated on the second. Once it was filled, he went on to the next bottles.

"Oh fuck!"

Whipping his head up, he looked at Kate. "What's wrong?"

"I tried to conjure a bottle of water." She held up a bottle. "It took me four tries to do it."

"Try again," he ordered, knowing his tone was probably harsh. As Kate tried again, Isaac continued to fill the other two bottles. The first one was fine, but the second one took him three tries.

Kate had two bottles of water in her hands. "No problems?"

"It took me several tries. It's like my magic is cutting in and out. It's not slow, it's just there one moment and not the next."

Isaac's normal sense of calm and patience felt like it was going to crack, but he held on. He wanted to be calm for Kate. They each had their strengths, and over the last week, they had found somewhat of a balance. She brought light, passion, and fun to their relationship whereas Isaac brought calm, reasoning, and practicality. Putting it that way sure made him sound like the boring one, but it worked for them. And right now, that balance really mattered if things were starting to go wrong.

He tightened the lid on the remaining water bottle and placed it in its designated spot on the shelf.

Doing a slow turn in the room, he tried to figure out what their next move should be. The shelving unit was on the same wall as the headboard, with the nightstand in between, so that wall was taken. But there was space in front of the shelving unit before the bins butted up next to the screen with the toilets. The last remaining space, besides the few feet to walk from the bed to the toilet, was the three feet at the base of the bed.

Having come to a decision, Isaac turned around and stopped. Kate sat on the bed, surrounded by ten or twelve small plastic water bottles.

"My magic is still cutting in and out." Kate's voice was shaky, and he could see the panic in her eyes.

Pushing aside the water bottles, he sat on the bed and pulled her into his lap. "I don't know what's going to happen, but we're going to make a plan. First, I think we should conjure another shelving unit." He pointed to the existing shelving unit in an attempt to get her to focus. "We can put it flush to the other one and only pull it out when we need something. Or leave enough space between the two to be able to reach an arm in."

"Okay. Then what?"

"I think we should conjure some big water jugs, maybe

five gallons a piece, and we can store them at the end of the bed."

"And food. And another toilet. No. Two."

He would have laughed if he wasn't so worried they were going to need it. Lifting her to her feet, he gave her a soft kiss. "Why don't you conjure the shelving unit and then start on the food? I'll work on the water."

She nodded and stepped toward the far wall, which was only a few feet away. "And don't forget another two toilets," she called over her shoulder.

Isaac moved to the end of the bed to conjure five-gallon water jugs, hoping they wouldn't need them.

Kate tried again to conjure a can of water-packed turkey, and this time, her magic worked. She was so exhausted, all she wanted to do was sit down and cry, but she needed to keep going.

"Hey, how you doing?" Isaac asked, coming up behind her in the small space. He kissed the back of her neck, and she closed her eyes, absorbing the attention. A few days ago, she'd conjured some dry shampoo, and now she kept her hair in a clip most of the time, which gave him full access to her neck.

She leaned back against him and let him take some of her weight. "I'm tired."

Taking her hand, he led her the few feet to the bed. "Me too. Let's sit down and eat something."

"No, we need to keep working," she protested but didn't resist as he gently pushed her so she was sitting on the bed. "My magic is cutting out for longer and longer. If we don't keep going, we won't have enough," she said quietly, too tired to even whine.

"We'll just take a little break since we missed dinner again. It's almost eight and we need to eat. Here." He put a bowl of steaming rice with chicken and a fork in her one hand and a bottle of water in the other. "It might be one of the last hot meals we get for a while, so enjoy."

Isaac hadn't said it, but they both knew it could be their last hot meal—ever. Exhaustion continued to pull at Kate, but she forced herself to eat, knowing she needed the fuel.

When their magic had started cutting out in the early afternoon, they began conjuring what they could. As time went on, their magic cut out more and more.

In the last hour or so, Kate had only been able to conjure a few items. That equaled to one or two days' worth of food if they were careful.

So wrapped up in her own exhaustion and fear, Kate had been relying more and more on Isaac for his support and encouragement as the day went on. Neither of them had said much as they had struggled with their magic. "How are you doing?" Kate asked between mouthfuls.

"I'm tired, but eating something will help. I've filled as many five-gallon jugs of water as we can fit in the space because we need to leave a little room. We'll have to have space to store waste, like the filled portable toilets," he said, nudging her shoulder.

"Eww, gross. And thanks for that," she teased, pushing his shoulder back. "I honestly didn't even think about that." Kate glanced up at the shelves she'd been working to fill. Even while creating the cans and boxes, it hadn't really dawned on her that they'd now have even more garbage. "It's all in packaging."

Isaac must have heard the despair in her voice as he

gave her shoulder another gentle nudge. "Hey, it'll be okay. We'll flatten the boxes and put them under the bed. That's why we purposely made it six inches off the ground, remember?"

That was the first time in her life she'd had to put so much thought into a bed. A good headboard, enough space, and comfy was all she'd ever considered before. Raising the bedframe too high would have meant even less headroom for Isaac when he was sitting on the bed and too low wouldn't have given them storage space underneath.

Every day, there was something more to consider in their tiny little world. She looked around the space and wondered how much more they could fit. And how many more air fresheners they would need. The place might be considered cozy if she played with the definition of the word, but daisy-fresh it wasn't.

"Are you finished?"

Kate looked down at her bowl and realized she'd eaten more than half. "Yes, thanks." She handed the bowl over for him to clean and walked back over to the shelves, taking stock of what they had.

They now had water to rehydrate food, but if their magic stopped working, they'd have nothing to heat the water. Eating cold, rehydrated, freeze-dried stew didn't sound all that appetizing.

The few perishables she'd created sat neatly on the shelves along with all the canned meats, crackers, peanut butter, honey, packages of instant foods, and various snacks. Trying to group meals in her mind to figure out what else they needed, she settled on more lunch-box size milk and juice containers that could be stored on a shelf.

Every so often, Isaac touched base with her to see how she was doing. A couple of months ago—hell, even a few weeks ago—that would have annoyed the hell out of her. Her first thought would have been that she didn't need someone constantly checking up on her. But now she knew Isaac wasn't doing that. He was checking *in*, not checking up. Because he cared. She wasn't sure when it had happened, but that one little word adjustment altered her outlook. Or maybe it was just Isaac.

She'd been working for a couple hours, and thinking about Isaac made her turn to look at him, appreciating everything he'd done for her.

The room shook and pitched her forward. Her shoulder hit the shelving units and packages fell all around her.

A cracking sound followed.

In the next instant, Isaac was right beside her, helping to upright the shelving units.

As soon as they were steady, he took her in his arms. "You okay?"

"I'm fine." She pulled back to see his face. "You?"

"I'm okay."

They both turned to survey the damage. Besides the packages from the shelves, the lantern and phone had fallen off the nightstand and the folding screen was tilted toward the wall.

"Nothing is broken," she said as she put the lantern and phone back in place.

"Kate? Remember the loud cracking sound?"

She looked where Isaac was pointing. "Oh, fuck." On the wall closest to the foot of the bed, there was a hairline crack. It ran from the floor to about three feet up. "Do you think that's a good thing? That the wall will crack open and we'll be able to get outside?"

"If this room was somewhere on the ground… maybe, but I'm not sure it is."

Slowly spinning around, she looked at everything they had lined up on the floor. Something had changed. "I thought the side of the bed and the headboard weren't touching the wall?" She turned back to Isaac, her eyebrows raised in question.

"No, there's about an inch gap."

"Not anymore."

Isaac did as she had just done, assessing the room. "The walls have moved."

"I'd just been hoping that the shaking knocked every-thing against the walls, but I think you're right. Every-thing on the floor is a little bit closer together." Moving over next to Isaac, Kate ran her palm along the crack and gasped. "I feel nothing."

"The malevolence is gone?"

Laying both palms flat on the crack, she closed her eyes. "No, I don't think so. Well… I'm not sure. I feel like something is missing inside me. I think my magic is gone. I can't sense anything."

Pulling her hand off the wall, she held it out, palm up, and tried to conjure a tissue. It was one of the first things all magic children were taught to conjure because it took very little magic. It should work even with her magic sputtering in and out. Her hand remained empty.

"Oh my god! It's gone!" She looked up at Isaac and when he shook his head, she knew his magic was gone too. She collapsed, dropping to her knees.

Isaac picked her up, and she clung to him as he sat on the bed, his hand cradling her head.

"We've known since this morning that we could lose our magic," he said quietly.

"I know... I guess... I didn't think I really believed it would happen. Even all day while we were conjuring, I thought it was just one of those things you do, like get fire insurance. But you don't really expect to have a fire... I... I've never been without my magic."

She rubbed her fingers against her chest, almost expecting to feel a gaping hole; the loss of her magic felt like a tangible crevice cut into her skin.

Isaac rocked her slowly back and forth, the minutes ticking away.

"Why don't you use the toilet and get ready for bed?" he asked as he moved her off his lap and stood. "I'm going to turn off two of the lanterns to preserve the battery life because we won't be able to charge them anymore."

Another sense of loss hit her as she stared up at him. "We won't even know what day it is."

Sitting back down, Isaac took her cheeks in his hands. "It's okay. We conjured a clock this afternoon, remember? I already set the date. It's December first, but it doesn't matter, because whatever day it is, we're going to be here when someone finds us."

Kate wanted to believe him. Believe they'd be found. But her hope was draining faster now. They'd been in the room eight days, and they had enough food and water for maybe a few weeks, but what if that wasn't long enough? What if no one ever found them? With the crack in the wall and the shifting, there were too many unknowns to know what the future held.

Isaac lifted Kate's hand away from the wall and tucked it under the blanket, snugging her closer while he spooned her body to keep her warm.

Even in her sleep, Kate's new obsession with touching the walls continued, as if she always hoped to feel something. But there was only the drywall and the cold.

It had been two weeks since they lost their magic. A total of twenty-two days in the room. Counting the days had become *his* obsession. Somewhere in his mind, he figured if he lost track of time—something that would be so easy to do in the room—he would lose track of reality.

Time had never really concerned him before. He had never worn a watch, but he had a clock on the wall in his shop out of necessity, and his phone was usually someplace close. His clients knew when to show up, and if they didn't, staring at the time wouldn't change anything.

To make sure he was never late for an appointment, he always set a couple of warning alarms on his phone. They

did the trick and allowed Isaac to focus on more important things than watching a clock.

Their recent loss of technology had changed the tide
for him. Once he knew that the batteries on the chargers
would eventually run out, he got the sense that he and
Kate were grains of sand in an hourglass. The glass
measured time in days or weeks instead of hours, but the
feeling was the same.

To add to the sense of doom, every couple of days,
new cracks formed in the walls. The walls continued to
creep inward, diminishing the room's size. Their space
used to be a ten-by-ten room, but now it was just a little
over seven-by-seven.

The walls sandwiched the bed from either end. What
was left of the full five-gallon jugs of water were now in
the middle of the room with the empties piled by the
shelves. To get to the toilet, they had to step over the
items crowded together on the floor.

A foul stench lingered in the air. The smells from the
toilets and food waste worsened a little each day. He and
Kate didn't smell like roses either, but it didn't bother him
as much as it did her. When she had her period, she had
tried to keep her distance from him. Not that it was
possible in their small space, but she said she couldn't
understand how he'd even want to touch her.

He couldn't help but smile thinking about all the
conversations they'd had recently, even the awkward
ones.

"I feel totally gross," Kate whined.

*Isaac pulled her closer. "Neither of us are clean and I don't
care. We're together, and that's all that matters. Just think of
this as an adventure and we're camping."*

Kate laughed. "If I was camping, I'd at least have hot coffee."

"Well..." He paused as if seriously thinking about camping. "We have lanterns and portable toilets. That's like camping."

She snorted a laugh. "I can't argue with that. But first I had my period—I mean, that's just nature, so it's not normally gross, but I want a shower. And I want to shave my legs and armpits. If we were camping, there'd be a shower."

"We might not smell clean, but you're still beautiful to me."

"Ahhh... you always know just what to say." She kissed him and ran her fingers through his beard.

"If you can handle this thick beard I've got going on, then the hair on your body is not going to bother me."

As fun as teasing had been, Isaac thought their state of cleanliness was the least of their worries. Even with rationing their food, they had eaten the last of it yesterday. He'd read somewhere once that the human body could survive without food for about three weeks, sometimes a month. But that depended on the person.

Kate hadn't been eating much before they lost their magic, and he worried she wouldn't last even two weeks without food. The thought of losing her was more than he could bear to contemplate. The fear was a living, breathing entity that beat inside him, louder than his heartbeat.

He knew a body could only survive without water for a few days at most. Luckily, they still had water, but the thought of running out had worsened Isaac's obsession with time and keeping track of the date. Checking the date had advanced from an obsession to a compulsion. Each time he woke, he looked at the clock to see if another day had passed.

December twenty-sixth. That was his new compulsion. December twenty-sixth. He'd taken to repeating the date again and again in his mind. That day would signal eleven days without food. If they were rescued before then, he believed Kate would have a chance.

As he lay in the near-dark huddled next to Kate, he kept his arms around her and one hand on her chest. He needed to feel the rise and fall of her breaths for his own peace of mind. They only used one lantern at a time now. The battery in one had died, leaving them with only two. They kept the setting on low, which allowed it to emit only a dim light, but Isaac wanted to conserve the battery. The chargers were almost drained, but they had them just in case.

When Kate stirred sometime later, she rolled onto her back. "Hey, my handsome tattooed lumberjack."

She'd started calling him her lumberjack a few days before. They had a small mirror Kate had conjured early on, but he didn't bother to look at himself. He figured he looked more like a scruffy homeless person than a hulking lumberjack, but if teasing him distracted her, she could call him anything she liked.

Rolling back a bit to reach beside the bed, he grabbed a bottle of water and passed it to her. "Here, have some water."

She took the bottle and pushed up to a sitting position, but she didn't drink. "Are you sure we have enough?"

"We're fine. Please drink."

When she'd drunk almost the entire bottle, he finished off what was left and put the bottle back on the floor.

They snuggled back under the covers, using them and

their body heat to get warm. The temperature in the room seemed to drop a little more each day. Going to the toilet now felt just like the camping adventure he'd tried to convince Kate to think of. That is, if they were camping in winter.

"Is it still the same day?" Kate asked in a whisper.

"Yes, still December sixteenth."

Kate palmed his cheek as their gazes met. "I love you, Isaac."

"I love you too, Turquoise." She told him a dozen times a day that she loved him, and he always said it back. He did love her, more than he ever thought possible, but he understood why she was telling him so often now. They both feared that one time they would say it would be the last time they had a chance.

He kissed her softly on the lips and she kissed him back, her hand moving around his neck. When they'd first lost their magic, she worried that her breath wasn't minty-fresh anymore. After he finally convinced her that it didn't matter because nothing on them was minty-fresh, she relaxed into his kisses again.

"I want to make love to you, Kate, my beautiful Turquoise."

She chuckled softly against his lips. "You're getting cornier every day."

Then she pulled back and her expression sobered. "We ran out of condoms... I could get pregnant."

He had to swallow to make sure he could get the words out against the tightness threatening to constrict his throat. "I'd be honored to make a baby with you, Kate. I love you with everything that I am. And if we made a baby, I would love them equally as much."

Kate's eyes became glassy, and she only nodded before she pulled him to her. His lips glided over hers before he deepened the kiss, but neither of them rushed. They had the time to savor each other.

Talking about making a baby was emotional, but it was what they didn't say that was overwhelming.

It was likely that if they did become pregnant, they would both die before the baby ever had a chance.

Isaac pushed all those thoughts out of his head because the only thing that was important at that moment was making love to Kate. To show her without words how much he loved her and to share his reassurances with her through his touch.

As their hands roamed under the blankets, they stretched out their kiss, taking their time. They'd foregone clothes a couple of weeks ago because there wasn't any point in wearing them. If they got out of bed, it was only to use the toilet or grab water, and then they were right back under the covers.

Moving down her body, Isaac trailed his lips and kisses over Kate's jaw and neck while his hands kneaded her breasts. She had lost weight since they'd been in the room, but he would love her body no matter what; if she gained weight, lost weight—it wouldn't matter.

Ducking his head under the blankets, he sucked one of her nipples into his mouth. She arched under him. His cock hardened where it rubbed against her thigh, creating a friction that was like sparks starting a warm smolder.

He lavished attention on both her breasts and then moved back up, knowing she didn't want him to kiss any lower. Regardless of where he kissed her, he would ensure he sparked a fire within her.

Gliding his lips over her chest and up her neck, he worked his way back up to her mouth. The cool air hit him as he emerged from the covers, but the warmth of Kate's kiss soon consumed him.

"I want to touch you," she whispered as he felt her hand snake between their bodies. A groan escaped his lips when she gripped him.

"Put me inside you," he demanded softly. He braced himself on either side of her, making sure his body and the blankets protected her from the cold air.

Kate guided him to her warmth, and when he felt her soft flesh against his, he pushed in slowly. "Oh fuck, you feel so good." With her tight heat surrounding him, he rocked forward. Slowly. Then he retreated just as slowly.

"More, Isaac. I need more."

"Let me take my time loving you, Turquoise." He stroked into her again, going deeper but not faster. In and out, he continued, keeping the pace slow until she was arching up against him, begging him for more.

Dropping to his elbows one at a time, he clasped Kate's hands. With their fingers linked and their bodies flush against each other, he continued to drive into her, deep and slow.

When he felt her body begin to tighten and his own orgasm rushing up on him, he kissed her while he continued to love her. His mouth made love to hers just as their bodies did.

"Yes!" she yelled against his mouth as he felt her arch once more, a burning igniting in them both. Their fire continued to build and their skin heated until Kate screamed his name as her body erupted with pleasure.

That was all it took for him to erupt with her, his orgasm hitting him like a burst of fireworks on a clear night.

When they cleaned up with their diminishing supply of wipes and were once more tucked under the blankets, he held her as she fell asleep.

"No matter what happens, Turquoise, I will love you until my last breath," he whispered into her hair.

18

Kate trailed her fingers along Isaac's chest as he leaned partially slouched against the headboard. He had one arm wrapped around her, holding her to his side. They had adopted the new position out of necessity.

The week before, to save space, they had laid the empty shelving units flat on the floor, one on top of the other. Needing them to store food was no longer an issue. They piled whatever they could balance on top of the units.

Even the portable toilets went on the stack. If they needed to use one, they'd take it down. That wasn't often anymore since they hadn't eaten in over a week.

Then, three days ago, a loud crack had split the air, and the bed shook, waking them from sleep. The bed rocked, heaving them forward and pushed against their feet.

Kate's heart had leapt to her throat for two opposing reasons, both equally as strong: the fear that the room was about to implode and the hope that they would be rescued battled against each other.

Forced into the middle of the bed as the headboard pushed inward, Kate held her breath as Isaac retrieved one of the lanterns. Shuffling on his knees, he moved down to the end of the bed to inspect the damage.

That was when fear won out, killing Kate's tiny spark of hope. The walls had moved. Again.

All four walls had contracted inward.

The wall the bed was against shoved the bed further into the cramped space, right up against the shelves and toilets.

Since the walls had already been crowding the bed from end to end, there was no room to be had when the walls pushed in.

The footboard collapsed and the bed buckled. What had once been a full-size bed was now a crunched and buckled frame less than six feet in length. Isaac could no longer sleep lying down. The only solution had been to pile pillows up against the end of the bed. Cushioning the buckle in the headboard made it bearable for them to lean against.

For the past three days, Kate wondered how she would die. Crushed to death by the contracting walls or her body eventually shutting down due to starvation? She'd gone over the scenarios in her mind a hundred times, and each time, she wondered whether she would have been better off accepting the option of being turned into a zombie. At least then there would have been hope that someone would find a way to stop Maverick and reverse the mind control.

During the moments of despair, she realized that for

as long as she lived—even if it was only a few more days—she would be grateful for the time she'd had with Isaac. For twenty-eight days, she had gotten to know and love him. She wouldn't trade that for anything.

Isaac shifted, bringing Kate out of her thoughts. "Drink please, Turquoise," he pleaded softly, handing her a bottle of water.

She took the water and sipped slowly, downing almost half of it before handing it back. "What about you?"

"I'll have the rest." He did as he said he would before placing the water bottle on the floor in the small space between the bed and the stacked shelving units.

Knowing she shouldn't but unable to ignore the compulsion, Kate rotated toward the wall and pulled her arm away from Isaac's warmth. Flattening her palm against the drywall, she closed her eyes, desperately wanting to feel something that would give her hope. Instead, the wall felt colder than it had been before. Just as the room was.

They could now see their breath.

Right after the most recent shift in the room, Kate had pushed on the wall and screeched, jerking her arm back, when she'd felt the wall move. For a moment, she feared it would crack and they would fall out into space... or wherever they were.

But instead of punching outward, the wall had moved inward a fraction more.

It still didn't stop her from needing to touch the wall. Without saying anything, Isaac took her hand and pulled it back to his chest, tugging her body against his warm skin. She knew she was obsessed with touching the wall—

hoping to feel something but not knowing what. Her magic returning, maybe.

They'd been without their magic for three weeks now. It felt like an eternity, with dying the only end she could see. She didn't say the words out loud to Isaac, but they both knew it.

They had been in the room for four full weeks. They hadn't eaten in a week, their water supply was running low, and the room was slowly crushing them.

Leaning down, she placed a kiss on Isaac's chest, then met his gaze. "I love you, Isaac." She couldn't remember how long it had been since she'd said it last, maybe hours, but she needed to make sure he knew.

"I love you too, Kate." He kissed the top of her head.

They stayed in each other's arms, her fingers slowly caressing his chest and his trailing over her arm. They hadn't made love in three days—their energy was waning, it was cold, and now they had very little room to move.

After only offering Isaac sex for months, she never expected that the act of them holding each other like they were could mean so much more. They had each other's love for however long they... She choked out a sob as a hard lump formed in the back of her throat. She didn't want to think about them dying, but it was becoming harder and harder to ignore.

"Hey," Isaac said as he lifted her onto his lap. She straddled him, thankful she still had enough headroom, and he pulled the blankets over her shoulders, tucking them in around them both. "What's wrong? Are you hurting?"

She shook her head, fighting against the desolation that had become a constant shroud enveloping them, but it was no use. Her tears finally let loose and spilled over.

Isaac's hand found its usual spot on the back of her neck, and he used his thumb to wipe away her tears. She loved that his fingers were so long they could span across so much of her skin. Although she couldn't feel where the tattoo climbed up her neck, she knew his palm covered it as his fingers caressed her cheek.

Taking in shallow breaths, she swallowed again, trying to get herself under control. "I was just thinking about the last time we made love."

"Well, if that made you cry, then I wasn't doing it right," he teased.

"What if we never—" She couldn't finish the sentence and choked on the last word, a sob bursting out of her.

Isaac pulled her against his chest, wrapping her tight in his arms. He didn't say anything for several minutes, but then, as if shoring up his own hope in order to reply, he said, "We have to believe that someone will find us."

Kate wasn't sure she could believe that anymore. She didn't think Isaac did either, but she didn't contradict him, letting that little bit of hope linger in the air.

He held her for the longest time, her hips straddling his, but she didn't have the energy for sex. She only needed to feel him. Sleep was threatening to pull her under when Isaac kissed her forehead.

"Merry Christmas, Turquoise. I love you."

She pulled back so she could look up into his eyes. "Merry Christmas, my lumberjack." They kissed softly. "I didn't think it was the twenty-fifth yet."

"It's not. It's December twenty-third. I just couldn't wait any longer to wish you a merry Christmas."

Isaac didn't look away from her, but she knew he was

lying. He didn't think they were going to live until Christmas Day—only two days away.

Weakness had become Kate's constant state of being. She slept more hours than she was awake, but she thought that was good because it conserved her energy.

Laying her head back on his chest, she wrapped her arms around his waist and listened to his heartbeat.

"Do you remember last Christmas?" he whispered. There was no reason to whisper, but they did it a lot, or they talked softly. Maybe they unconsciously didn't want to make too big a wave out into the universe and have the room dissolve. If they were quiet, they could stay wrapped in each other's arms a little longer, hoping for someone to rescue them.

"Yes. It was a pretty sad Christmas. The first one without Beatrice and Elise, and with Reece getting worse every day. But everyone tried to put on a good face for Christmas day."

"They did. And do you remember the gift exchange?"

She smiled against his chest. "Of course. We hadn't known each other long, but I bought you a lovely candle."

"Is that what you're going with?" She could hear the smile in his voice, and it warmed her.

"Yes. It was vanilla, I think."

"It was."

"And it was in a lovely jar," she said with an air of innocence. She loved dragging this out.

He brought his mouth to her ear and gave her a small kiss. "Do you remember what it said?"

She giggled. "Yes, *Thanks for All the Orgasms* in large black letters with a heart underneath."

"And you totally enjoyed me unwrapping it in front of your friends and family."

She giggled again, the sound so unlike her. "Well... I was *very* thankful." Isaac's gift to her had been practical and thoughtful—beautiful silver welder pencils. She was still using them. But just thinking about the candle made her smile.

They were quiet again for a while, and then Isaac reached over the side of the bed and got them some more water. When he turned off the light, it plunged them into total darkness, but it wasn't scary like it had been in the beginning. As long as she could feel Isaac's heartbeat against her cheek while she straddled his lap, his arms around her, she knew he would protect her.

"Although this wouldn't have been where I chose to spend Christmas," he whispered, "there is no one else I would want to spend Christmas, or any other holiday with. I love you, Kate."

"I love you, Isaac." She knew he would hear the tears in her voice, but it didn't matter. If life had turned out differently, she would have wanted to spend every future holiday with him too. Unfortunately, life wasn't always kind. She knew she wasn't going to get her wish.

PAIN HAD BECOME Isaac's constant companion. It had been nine days now without food, but it wasn't hunger pangs that threatened to drive him insane. Those had been uncomfortable and annoying but had ended over a week ago.

Muscle cramping had become Isaac's new torture. One he endured over and over again.

They started with a pull—his leg or his arm contracting without warning. Then his hand or foot would jerk as his muscles shortened and contracted. Lastly, pulses of electricity shot along his limbs, playing with his nerves like they were strings on a violin. The intense cramping in other muscles—back, neck, and stomach—was equally as brutal, but all he could do was breathe through them.

With the bed buckled, he couldn't lie flat, and with the ceiling too low for him to stand, Isaac hadn't straightened his body in over a week. Add in the lack of water, and it was the perfect recipe for suffering.

Shifting Kate gently in his arms, Isaac scooted his hips over to the edge of the bed and lowered his feet to the floor. Pushing his bare feet along the freezing wood, he stretched until his toes collided with items piled in the cramped space. It gave him minor relief, but it was better than nothing.

When the cold threatened to undo any good the stretching may have given him, Isaac shifted back onto the bed and under the blankets. Making sure Kate was covered, he settled back against the buckled headboard.

He picked up one of the water bottles he'd left on the bed between their bodies and the wall for easy reach. Placing the bottle between his raised knees and trying not to squeeze it, he used his hand that wasn't holding Kate to unscrew the top.

"Kate, drink for me," he urged as he placed the lip of the bottle on her cracked bottom lip and tipped it up slowly. A few drops dripped down her chin, but her eyes never opened. Then her survival instincts took over and she swallowed several mouthfuls. Isaac let out a breath of relief.

When he held the bottle up to his own dried lips, his tongue stiff, he had to force himself not to chug down what remained. No matter how thirsty he was, or how often his muscles twisted with agony, Isaac made sure Kate had most of the water.

If they were lucky, their remaining water supply would last until the next evening. December twenty-sixth.

Recapping the bottle, he laid it beside them and shifted back and forth on the pillows to find the least painful position. As he settled Kate more firmly against his chest, she let out a sigh in her sleep and burrowed into his warmth.

With the remaining lantern set on low, he had enough light to see Kate's face. He ran his fingers along her hair-line, pushing back the hair that had fallen forward. The clip from her hair had been discarded days ago, so her tresses fell around her shoulders and over his arms.

In the two days since they wished each other a merry Christmas, Kate had mostly slept. Isaac had done his fair share of sleeping as well, but the cramping jarred him awake at least once an hour. Although he could have done without the pain, it worked better than an alarm clock to make sure he checked on Kate.

The alarming rate with which she had weakened and the amount of time she slept terrified him. If he was honest, he'd been terrified from the moment Kate had been sucked through the wall of his shop. The relief he'd felt when they'd landed in the room and he realized his magic worked had only been temporary.

He'd told Kate that Ben and Sam had seen them get sucked through the wall, but he wasn't sure what they had seen. Or what Maverick was capable of manipulating. Making someone believe they saw something different than what they had seemed like child's play compared with turning people into zombies. And Maverick excelled at controlling people.

Isaac hunkered down into the mattress as much as the cramped space would allow. He maneuvered Kate so she was straddling him, and she moaned softly as he rested her head on his chest, giving his arms a bit of a break. He would move her again in a little while, making sure she didn't stay in one position for too long. Anything he could do to lessen her muscles cramping, he would.

In the meantime, he let his mind wander.

Austin had been in his thoughts a lot during the last month. Not that he was ever far from them. Yet talking about him with Kate had brought memories of Austin to the forefront and telling the story of his death had Isaac looking at it with a different lens. Or maybe it was facing death that had him reevaluating what had happened.

After Austin's death, Isaac had been determined to never hurt anyone again. To do that, he had chosen to make all tattoo decisions himself. He hadn't given Kate or Isabella the opportunity to decide whether they wanted to take a risk on their tattoos because he'd taken their choices from them.

He'd been so sure that by making the choices himself, he could prevent hurting anyone. Yet, if he hadn't given in to Austin, he would have hurt him anyway, because Austin would have come to resent him. Would he have gotten depressed regardless? Was his suicide always fated to happen?

Maybe Kate would have come to resent him too. Would she have also turned to suicide because of her pain? That was a question no one could answer, not even Kate.

When Damon had listened to Isaac's story about what happened with Austin's tattoo, he'd asked whether the person, meaning Austin, had understood the risks. Isaac admitted that even he hadn't known the risks. As if somehow he should have known everything that could happen in life. When had he become so arrogant to think he knew or could predict everything?

That's what he was—arrogant. He'd accused Kate of being a coward because she tried to protect herself by running from her feelings. Isaac had done the exact same thing—act like a coward—but instead of running, he'd used his arrogance as a crutch so he wouldn't have to let someone make a decision he thought was dangerous.

Not for the first time during the last month, he wondered what would have happened if he had tattooed Kate sooner. Sure, the tattoo was meant to help her deal with the magic embedded in the sword, but since it was for protection, could it have helped her deflect Maverick's magic? Another question they'd never know the answer to.

Canting his head to the side, he watched Kate's face as she rested against his chest while she slept. He wanted to be able to watch her every day. Wake up with her every morning until they were both old and gray. Had he been so arrogant and thoughtless in his life that this was his punishment? Not only would he lose the only woman he had ever loved, but would he have to watch the life drain out of her as her life was cut short along with his?

They'd survived so much in the thirty days they'd been trapped in their box. Each time they faced a new challenge, he thought he couldn't be more terrified. Then something else would get thrown in their path that showed him how wrong he'd been.

In the past few days, Kate had become more and more difficult to rouse from sleep, and the thought that eventually she would never wake again sent a new terror coursing through him. It forced him to realize that he'd still been clinging to a tiny bit of hope after all. Then it died.

They were going to die in this room, and he wouldn't be able to live even an hour without her. He would love her until his last breath, and when she took her last before him, his would follow right after.

He lifted her higher up on his chest, bringing their faces closer together. Then he closed the few inches between them and glided his lips over hers. "Merry Christmas, Kate. My turquoise," he whispered.

His voice caught in his throat, and he swallowed as he felt tears slide down his cheeks. "I love you and I will for eternity."

He kissed her again and held her tight as sleep dragged him under.

19

Isaac's heart swelled with love as he watched Kate run through the high grass. She laughed, the carefree sound floating toward him. The air was cool for the early September morning, but it made for a perfect day to be outside. The sun felt warm on his face, and he welcomed the sensations, thinking it had been far too long since he'd felt them.

The wildflowers were still in full bloom, the bright pinks and purples adding splashes of color to the green grass. The mountains towered in the distance as if protecting all below them.

As Kate ran, her hair flowed behind her like a cape caught in the wind. She slowed and turned around before walking backward, smiling at something. Isaac's gaze tracked her path. He'd been so enraptured with Kate, he hadn't noticed the little boy, maybe two years old, who toddled after her. His short legs were mostly hidden in the tall grass as he followed.

Kate held out her hand, and a sword appeared. It was

long and silver with a simple design spiraling around it. Without looking closely, Isaac knew it was made of rubber. Crouching down, Kate passed the sword to the toddler. His laughter bubbled up, innocent and cheerful as he grasped the rubber hilt.

As the boy swung the sword over his head, Kate conjured another one. Adopting the voice of an evil witch, she pretended to cackle and warned the boy to run. He laughed and almost toppled over in his excitement. After steadying him, she stepped back and cackled again, encouraging him to run.

Catching on to the game, the boy held his sword in front of him and toddled as fast as his little legs would take him. Kate closed in on him, continuing to cackle and talk in her witchy voice.

The little boy looked back at her, laughing with joy. Then his sword caught in the grass, and he stumbled forward.

Isaac's heart clenched before he let out a breath as Kate picked up the boy. She held him high above her face, her dress flattening against her rounded belly with the action, as she blew a raspberry on his neck.

In some far recess of his mind, Isaac knew the sight before him was a dream. He was only a bystander, watching a wish of what could never be.

"Isaac!"

He turned, looking for the person who had called his name.

Far off in the distance, he could see Kate's house and her workshop. A woman stepped out from the shadows of the building. Something about her seemed familiar, but he turned away since he yearned to watch Kate with the little boy.

"Isaac! Isaac!" the woman continued to call to him. Her voice had taken on an urgent tone, sounding closer now.

Forcing himself to tear his gaze away from Kate and the toddler once more, he turned back to the woman.

"Isaac, can you hear me?"

"Yes," he said, wondering why she would ask such a question when he was standing only a few feet away.

"Do you know who I am?"

He squinted as if that would help him see her better in the morning sun. "Fiona?"

"Oh, thank god! Isaac, I need you to wake up."

He glanced over his shoulder again, catching a glimpse of Kate. If he woke from the dream, then Kate would disappear.

"Isaac!" Fiona called again, louder this time. "Listen to me. You need to wake up. If you don't wake up, this dream will never come true!" Her voice choked on the last word before she continued. "Please, honey, wake up," she pleaded.

Isaac's eyes flung open.

The pitch-black of the room disoriented him after the glorious Colorado sun. It took a moment for Isaac to come back to the present. The lantern's battery must have died while he slept, leaving the room shrouded in complete darkness.

His arms were stiff and cramped where he held Kate; he hadn't let her go, even in sleep. She felt so still against his chest. When the realization of what that meant registered in his exhausted brain, a new fear gripped him.

He needed to see her smile, like he had in the dream. If only the total darkness could let up, for even a moment.

"Kate?" His voice was barely audible, even to his own ears. He tried to clear his throat but choked on the dryness. Taking a deep breath and then forcing himself to swallow, he tried again. "Kate? Can you hear me, Turquoise?"

Holding her against his chest, he felt for the rise and fall of her own. The panicked thump of his own heartbeat confused him. He couldn't tell if he was feeling himself or Kate.

Bending forward, he put his ear near her mouth. When a soft puff of air hit his cheek, he huffed out a dry laugh of joy. The feel of her breathing meant they still had time. But how much?

Isaac?

He reared up at the sound of his name and scanned the room, as if expecting to suddenly be able to see in the darkness. Had he gone back to sleep? Was he hallucinating?

Closing his eyes, he tried to picture the field of wildflowers behind Kate's house again so he could see Kate and the little boy laughing.

But behind his eyelids, there was only more blackness.

Isaac?

He heard his name again. Only this time, he knew the voice hadn't come from inside the room. It had been spoken in his head. It must be a hallucination—there was no magic in the room. Or maybe it was a vision, like Fiona from the dream.

Isaac, can you answer me?

He closed his eyes as exhaustion pulled at him. He wanted to return to the dream with Kate.

Isaac! Answer me! The voice sounded frantic now.

Afraid to hope what the voice might mean, Isaac ran his hands over Kate. The feel of her gave him the strength to reach out to the voice.

For the first time in weeks, he pulled on his magic. Even though it was faint and weak, it was a welcome feeling inside himself.

Yes? he answered the voice.

It's Jack. We're coming for you.

Isaac wanted to believe the voice was real. That his mind wasn't playing tricks on him. Tiny sparks of hope lit deep in his soul as his eyes burned with tears his body was too dry to create.

Isaac? Are you still there?

Yes.

We can't find a way in. We need you to help us.

Isaac opened his eyes as wide as he could but was met with the only inky blackness.

How? he asked, the familiarity of his magic coming back, even in its weakened state.

Then he croaked a dry laugh. Magic. He had his magic. Tightening his hold on Kate with one arm, he held out his other hand just as he had thirty days ago and used his magic. A small ball of light appeared for a moment before it fizzled out. He tried again, concentrating on making the smallest ball of light he could.

We need an opening.

In part of his mind, Jack's answer registered, but Isaac didn't respond as he focused on the light.

Setting the tiny ball of light on the blanket, Isaac

brushed Kate's hair off her face while he continued to hold her against his chest. Even in the dim light, he could see flaky patches on Kate's dry, pale skin. Her lips were dry and cracked too, patches of blood caked into the edges where they had split.

Pulling on his magic, Isaac tried to conjure a bottle of water, but he was too weak. He tried three times, and each time, he felt himself growing weaker. When he gave up, despair punched him hard.

Isaac?

Isaac!

Isaac bent forward and kissed Kate's forehead. When he straightened, he knew he needed to respond to Jack.

I'm here.

You have to help us! We need an opening.

Isaac barked a harsh laugh, then coughed as the sound stuck in his throat. An opening? If only it were that easy.

Kate let out a large, shuddering breath like she was expelling her last one just as his magic light sputtered and died, pitching the room into darkness.

Panic seized Isaac as he fumbled for her shoulders in the dark. He gripped her upper arms and yanked her up higher onto his chest. With one arm wrapped around her, he gently prodded her with his fingers, trying to find her mouth. Lowering his face to her mouth, he froze, waiting for her soft puff of breath.

It felt like a century passed by before he felt the small breath. He didn't move as he waited for another one. When it finally came, he realized they were coming too far apart.

Hurry! he yelled into Jack's mind.

The room won't let us in! Isaac could feel Jack's frustration in his mind. *We need a way in!*

Isaac wanted to yell at Jack, and if he had the strength, he might have. Didn't Jack know that he and Kate wouldn't have been stuck in the fucking room for thirty days if there had been a goddamned opening?

His own breathing felt shallow now, and he panted as he lowered Kate to the blankets beside him. Trying to calm himself, he closed his eyes since he couldn't see in the dark anyway. Isaac knew the room. He knew every crack in the four walls, had studied them all.

Pushing up to his knees, his muscles shaking and barely strong enough to hold him, Isaac leaned over Kate and pressed both his palms to the wall. Dragging his hands around in circles, he searched for the large crack he knew was there.

It had formed right after the walls encroached further into the room, buckling the bed. Kate had pushed at the wall, and another crack tore through it. They had feared the wall would split open, and if they could have ensured they wouldn't tumble into space, they would have forced it.

Isaac knew this was his last hope.

He sent one final message to Jack: *Watch the walls.* Then he threw the last of his strength against the crack in the wall and pushed.

20

Isaac felt the wall vibrate under his palms, the crack's jagged edge tearing into his flesh. Fearing the entire structure would come crashing down, he gave the wall one final push. Then, forcing himself to find the strength, he curled his body backward and draped himself over Kate.

As he wrapped his arms around Kate's head, a deafening roar split the air.

With the force of a nine out of ten on the Richter scale, the room rocked from side to side. Still curled around Kate, Isaac felt their bodies go airborne. They were tossed into a solid object, barely giving him time to register the pain before they hurled backward like a boomerang.

Defenseless against the assault, Isaac curled further around Kate, desperate to protect her.

The room stopped moving, and a breeze fluttered across Isaac's naked back.

The sound of voices was the first thing to penetrate his mind, then he noticed the light.

Before he had a chance to get his bearings, Kate was pulled from his arms.

"Kate!" he yelled, but his words were only a soft whisper.

Hands clamped down on his arm, and Isaac tried to wrench it free. Without even the strength to bat away a fly, he was no match for the grip holding him.

In the rational part of his mind, buried deep below his fear and exhaustion, Isaac knew the hold on him was there to help. But the loss he felt from not holding Kate wasn't rational. Did she die? Was that the reason they took her away from him?

Closing his eyes, he tried to picture the dream with Kate and the little boy, then let his body go limp.

Something warm wrapped around him, but it wasn't like the sun in the field. A blanket? He wanted to feel the warmth of the sun and see Kate laughing amongst the wildflowers.

When someone tugged on Isaac again, he gave in. In the next moment, he felt like he was floating. Then his bare feet were lowered to some grass. Was he in the field? The grass was cool and soft against the pads of his feet. The blades felt short, like a manicured lawn, not like tall, wild grass in the field.

Muffled noises surrounded him, like voices yelling from a great distance. It was dark but not like it had been in the room. He blinked repeatedly, hoping to bring his vision into focus. When he looked up, he realized it was nighttime. Had another day passed?

Jack? Isaac threw out the question as someone helped him sit. A hand on his shoulder pushed him backward so he would lie down. Too weak to resist, he allowed it. His back muscles protested as they stretched out fully for the first time in a week. Or maybe longer. Isaac didn't know what day it was.

December twenty-sixth! Was that the date? It couldn't be because then the rescue would be too late. He tried to sit up, the compulsion to know the date propelling him, but someone pushed him back down.

Jack? he asked again.

We're here, Jack answered. *Let Meredith heal you.*

Healing could wait; he needed to know what day it was. *What's the date?* he asked Jack.

December twenty-fifth.

Isaac blew out a breath and settled back onto the grass. Christmas Day. They'd made it.

Isaac threw his hands up, covering his ears. He'd been drifting off to sleep when loud voices bombarded him from all angles, like someone had turned the volume up high. The sounds were painful in their intensity, and then they stopped.

"Sorry. You should be fine now."

Slowly, Isaac opened his eyes to see Meredith hovering above him. "Kate?" he asked. His voice still sounded rough, but it was a bit louder than before.

"She's going to be fine. Mirek and Jack are healing her. Fiona and I were healing you, but I didn't realize your hearing was damaged when the wall fell. Then, well..." She shrugged and gave a sheepish smile. "I guess I amplified it too much when I fixed it."

He struggled to get up, his need to get to Kate driving him.

"Not yet," Meredith said as if sensing his growing panic. "Kate is being well taken care of."

"I must see her."

"I get that, but just give yourself a few minutes." Meredith didn't wait for his answer, obviously assuming he would follow his take-charge friend. "Now that you're healed, let's start with getting you to sit up. Okay?"

Hands landed on him, and though he didn't know who they belonged to, they helped him into a sitting position. "Lean back against the tree," Meredith said. "You're going to be really weak for a while."

"Let me," a deep voice said beside him, and he turned to see Damon.

For an entire month, it had been just him and Kate. The sudden change was overwhelming. There were people everywhere touching, helping, and all the noise was disorienting.

Could this be what Kate felt like when people told her what to do? He tucked away the thought, making a promise to remember the feeling whenever Kate started to push back.

Holding onto Damon's arms, he allowed himself to be lifted backward until he leaned against the tree. He felt as weak as a newborn.

A hand squeezed his shoulder. "You heard me," Fiona said quietly, her voice filled with emotion.

Isaac turned and met her gaze; tears pooled in her eyes as she smiled softly. "You heard me," Fiona repeated.

His brain slowly pieced everything together. "You... you were in my dream."

"No," she said with a watery laugh. "You were in my vision. We'll explain it all tomorrow," she said before patting his shoulder. Reaching up, she took Damon's hand and he pulled her to her feet.

"Isaac."

The hesitancy in Meredith's voice had him tearing his gaze from Fiona and looking at her.

"You should look around and see where you are. I think it will come as a shock because it was to us."

Isaac looked past Meredith and noticed a familiar park bench. That couldn't be right.

"Help me up," he said, holding his hand out to Meredith. She hesitated for only a moment before pulling him to his feet. When he tilted to the right, he reached out a hand for support.

"I don't think standing is a good idea yet." She conjured a folding chair and pushed him into it.

As much as he wanted to protest, he didn't have the strength. Once more, he got a sense of what Kate must feel when he took control. Pushing the thoughts aside, he looked at the landscape in front of him.

The park bench was familiar because he could see it from his shop's front window. The lampposts edging the park cast enough light for him to see the three Williams buildings across the street. If they were that close…

He shifted in the chair to scan the area to his left. A line of people stood on the sidewalk, evenly spaced apart like trinkets on a shelf. Each person held their hands in front of them, but their hands were empty. Many of them were talking and laughing, implying they weren't Maverick's zombies.

"What's with them?" he asked Meredith, lifting his chin toward the line of people.

"They're holding a spell to block non-magics from seeing in." She crouched down in front of him like she was about to address a child. "Look, Isaac. I expect you're weaker than you realize. Since Kate is almost healed, we'll take you two to your apartment so you can rest. But before you go, I need you to see something before it's destroyed. Everything else we can explain tomorrow when you and Kate are up to it."

When Meredith stood and pointed, Isaac looked in the direction she indicated. His gaze landed on Kate first. Something settled in him when he saw her sitting up, talking to her mom.

Then he spotted what was above her head. "Holy fuck," he muttered.

Floating about ten feet off the ground was the room, or what was left of it.

Isaac could see the bed and their stacked pile behind it through the gaping hole where a wall had once been. Someone had lit the room's interior, highlighting the cracks and buckles in the structure. Looking at it from the outside sent a shiver down his spine. The room was no longer a room at all, only a tiny, cramped space.

He turned his head from side to side to look at the outside of the walls and couldn't understand what he was seeing. "Is the room in something?"

"We think so. Sam believes it's in another dimension. We didn't even know it was there. We... I'm so sorry, Isaac."

Drawing his gaze away from the crumbled prison, he looked at Meredith, hating the guilt and sorrow he heard in her voice. "You got us out; that's all that matters."

She nodded. "Ready to get Kate?"

"Yes." Looking back, he watched Jack walk around the room to face the hole in the front. His voice carried on the night air as he instructed half a dozen people to disappear all the items inside.

"Our drawings," he said in a panic. They represented more than just the sketches they contained. They told a story of the time they'd fallen in love.

"Pardon?" Meredith asked. "You need something?"

"Yes. There are two sketchbooks in the room. Can you ask Jack to save them?"

"Sure, I'll be right back."

Isaac must have zoned out because it felt like only a moment later that Meredith was back, and she wasn't alone. Reece helped Isaac to his feet just as Damon came over, cradling Kate in his arms. Isaac wished he could be the one carrying her.

Perhaps Damon understood because he brought his sister closer so Isaac could kiss her. "I love you, Turquoise," Isaac whispered.

"I love you too, my lumberjack."

There were a few chuckles. "I'm looking forward to hearing how those nicknames came about," Reece teased.

"Me too," Fiona said, "but later. For now, let's get them to Isaac's apartment."

Once they reached the apartment, everyone said their goodbyes except for Fiona, Damon, and Morgana.

Fiona ushered them all into the apartment and got Isaac and Kate settled on the couch.

"I'm sure you probably both want a shower, but since we cleaned you magically, please wait until tomorrow. You're both weak, and I'll worry if I think you're going to try standing in a slippery shower stall."

Isaac felt Kate sit straighter as if to protest, and Fiona must have seen it too.

"Kate, please. Give me this," Fiona begged softly.

Like a pin in a balloon, Kate deflated against his side as she sunk into him. "Okay. Tomorrow."

"Good." Fiona glanced briefly at Damon and Morgana before looking back at him and Kate. Isaac got the feeling that whatever Fiona was going to say had something to do with the dream. No... not a dream. She said it was a vision.

"We'll all meet at The Magic Plate tomorrow at noon to discuss the last month. But before we go, I want to say two things."

Fiona walked up to the couch and bent down to give Kate a kiss on the cheek. "Merry Christmas! I didn't think I was ever going to get to say..." Her words trailed off, and Kate wrapped her arms around her mom.

"I love you and merry Christmas," Kate whispered before letting her mom go. "What's the second thing?"

"You're pregnant with my grandson."

KATE WOKE SLOWLY, feeling Isaac's warmth where she lay half-draped over him. She had come to crave his warmth, and not just because the room had always been cold. It was the connection to him that she needed. She ran her fingers slowly along his chest, and even with her eyes closed, she could perfectly envision the tattoo inked there. Each feather, the dark and the shadows, she could trace without looking.

"Good morning, Turquoise," Isaac said quietly.

"Good morning." She placed a kiss on his chest, then

tilted her chin up as she opened her eyes to look into his. "Please tell me I'm not dreaming."

"It's real." He rolled toward her, shifting her onto her back. "That was my first thought when I woke up too. The curtains are drawn, but the sunlight was enough to make me think I was dreaming."

"We're pregnant," she whispered. They were going to have a baby.

That the news came from her mom was a shock. No peeing on a stick for her. She shouldn't have been surprised, not really, but she was. Her mom had always had visions, but the fact that her mom knew about the baby before she and Isaac did seemed strange.

"Yes, we are. You've made me the happiest man in the world. I want to talk all about the baby, but right now..." His voice trailed off as he hovered over her and dropped his lips to hers in the softest of kisses. Their tongues tangled together in a slow exploration as she ran her hands over his hips and his back. At first, neither of them hurried it along.

After a while of gentle kisses and caressing touches, Kate wanted more. She wanted to make love to Isaac and take him deep into her body. To remind herself they belonged together.

She lifted her hands to his face, running her fingers through his beard and into his hair. Tugging on the long strands at the nape of his neck, she pulled him down and deepened the kiss. He groaned into her mouth, igniting her passion even higher.

Kate's love and need for Isaac had grown each day to a point where she knew she'd never be sated.

Shoving at his chest, she pushed him onto his back.

She wanted to kiss every inch of him in the bright light of the morning.

When he moaned in a way that didn't sound at all sexy, she froze. "Did I hurt you?"

"I'm okay. My back muscles are just tight. I think they're still not used to being stretched and wanted to protest."

She felt a flash of guilt for all he'd endured for her. Even when Isaac could no longer fully stretch out in the room, he'd had Kate drape across him so she could. He'd also given her more water than he took for himself. He may not have flaunted the actions, but she'd known and loved him all the more because of it.

"We should probably eat," she said, looking up to meet his eyes. As much as she wanted to make love with Isaac, he was right. They were weak. If they didn't fuel their bodies, it would take them longer to get their strength back. Not to mention their magic.

She rolled off Isaac and scooted to the edge of the bed, hanging her legs over the side. Glancing back over her shoulder at him, she winked. "Come on, let's get something to eat and then a shower. Even though we're clean, I'd love to take one."

When she pushed to her feet, she realized too late that she should have tested the waters. Her knees buckled, and she cried out as she fell forward onto her hands.

"Kate?" Isaac's panicked cry came before he landed on the floor beside her.

"Isaac!" She tilted sideways, tumbling into him. "Are you okay?"

Laughing, he wrapped an arm around her, pulling her

onto his chest. "Yes, I'm fine. I slid off the bed on purpose."

"Why would you do that?"

He grinned. "I thought it was the fastest way to get to you. Since your legs didn't want to hold you, I figured mine wouldn't want to hold me either."

"You're nuts."

"I'm nuts about you."

She groaned. "Oh, that's *so* bad. I think your lines are getting worse, but I love you anyway." Brushing her lips over his, she aimed for a light kiss. But Isaac had a different idea, and several minutes passed before they came up for air.

Since neither of them were fast or steady on their feet, another few minutes passed before they were dressed. Kate wore a pair of Isaac's sweatpants and a T-shirt.

"It might take me awhile to get used to clothes again." She grinned at him. "No bra or panties."

He took her hand as they walked toward his kitchen. "Easy access."

She laughed. "Maybe so, but after the portable toilet and being naked together for weeks, I'm definitely not shy around you anymore."

Leaning down, he gave her a quick kiss. "You shouldn't be." Then he grinned. "And later, we can go back to being naked. But first, food."

Kate felt like it took her twice as long to walk to Isaac's kitchen as it should have. She was surprised, but she pushed the thought to the side as soon as she saw the huge buffet of food spread out on his island. "My mom definitely came through for us, but after not eating for ten days, we'll be lucky to eat more than a few bites. That's even after being healed."

Kate hoisted herself onto a stool and took one of the plates.

"You're eating for two, remember?"

She hadn't forgotten. Not even for a second since her mom told her.

Picking up a grape, she popped it into her mouth; the wet burst of flavor on her tongue tasted delicious. She ate a few more as thoughts of a baby rattled around in her mind. A baby boy. Would he look like her? Or Isaac? Would he have artistic talent like them?

It had been a long time since she had thought about having children. After Ethan, she figured it would never happen. Placing her hand on her stomach, she tried to imagine a baby growing inside. Since she had conceived less than two weeks ago, the baby would only be the size of a pinhead, but she loved him already.

Isaac turned toward her and placed his hand over hers. "What are you thinking?"

"Do you remember what you said in the room?"

He nodded, not even asking which part she meant. "Yes. Every word. I said I would be honored to make a baby with you, Kate. I love you with everything that I am. And if we made a baby, I would love them equally as much."

"Do you still believe that?"

His eyes shone with tears, but she knew they were happy tears. "Yes. I meant every word, and I already love him." He rubbed his hand over hers and then put some eggs and more fruit on her plate. "Eat, please."

"Everyone is so bossy," she teased but picked up her fork.

They each kept a hand on her belly. It made eating a little awkward, but neither of them seemed to care. She liked him touching her, and it felt right as they lapsed back into silence. Kate had grown so used to Isaac and periods of quiet together that she didn't feel the need to speak.

By the time they had finished eating and put the leftovers away, Kate was dreaming about her shower.

"I want toothpaste," she declared, taking the tube out of the holder and the toothbrush Isaac had conjured for her months ago even though she hadn't stayed often. "I haven't tried to use my magic yet, but I just need to taste the toothpaste in my mouth. Does that make sense?"

"It does." He waved his hand toward the shower, using magic to turn on the water before grabbing his own toothbrush. Standing in front of the mirror brushing their teeth together felt so domestic, something she would have run from before the room.

"Life before the room, and life after the room," she said after she rinsed her mouth. "I think that's how I'll always think of our *little adventure.*"

"In the summer, we can go camping and conjure a portable toilet and a camping lantern. We can even have freeze-dried food."

"Oh, you're so funny, my lumberjack," she said dryly as she gave him a shove. "Get in the shower."

They were both laughing as they got in. Then Kate's laughter turned to a groan as the water sluiced over her head and down her back. "Fuck. That's the most amazing feeling ever."

"Really? The most ever? I think that's a dare." With his hands on his hips, Isaac switched their positions. Standing under the spray, he got himself wet. Then he backed her up until her back was against the wall, his hands flat against the glass on either side of her head. He lowered his head ever so slowly. Her breathing sped up in anticipation, waiting for the first touch of his lips. The kiss was slow and easy.

But she didn't want slow and easy, and not because she wanted it to be impersonal like before. "Isaac, I need you. It feels like forever." She went up on her toes and nipped his lower lip. "Please."

"Please what? What do you want, Kate?"

His words were so much like the ones he'd uttered over six weeks ago in this very same shower. It was her words that were different this time. "Please make love to me, Isaac."

He looked her in the eyes, and she couldn't tear her gaze away from the love she saw there. He skimmed the back of his fingers over her chest and down her belly before slipping them between her legs.

His other hand wrapped around her waist and he tugged her close. Wet skin against wet skin. He kissed her as his finger slipped inside her. First one, and then two.

Keeping the kiss slow, his lips glided softly over hers. In direct contrast to his lips, his fingers moved faster and deeper, then his thumb circled her clit. His fingers took her higher and higher. And just when she thought she couldn't take it anymore, her body tightened and her back arched against his arm that was holding her. She called out his name as her body lit up inside like a thousand suns and then burst with the pleasure that only Isaac could give her.

When she finally came back to earth, she opened her eyes to see him smiling. Reaching up, she cupped his cheek to pull his mouth back to hers, but he resisted. "What's wrong? That was amazing, but I still want to make love to you."

"We will, but not in the shower. Let's wash off."

Kate took a deep breath and let it out slowly, willing herself not to get angry or jump to a conclusion. "Isaac?"

"Hmm?" he mumbled as he grabbed the bodywash and the scrubby thing.

"Uh… why can't we make love in the shower?"

Once he had a good lather on the scrubby thing, he began washing her shoulders and moving it down her arms, then onto her legs. "You can't just go with the flow? You're really going to make me mention it when we're naked together?"

"Mention what?"

He sighed, but when he lifted his eyes, she saw amusement twinkling there. "Your mom. Her concerns about us in the shower and doing something to harm her grandchild?"

"Oh my god!" A laugh burst from her. "You're right. No mentioning my mom when we're naked. Finish up there, my lumberjack, and let's get back to the bed."

21

*I*saac stopped Kate by wrapping his arm around and her and pulling her against him. "Are you sure you're okay? Not lightheaded?"

"I'm good." She brushed her lips against his, then linked their fingers. "I promise." They'd had a busy morning—eating, showering, making love in bed, showering again—and now flashing from his apartment to the hallway in the back of The Magic Plate. It was more activity than they'd done at once in a month.

Even with Kate's reassurance that she was okay, there were too many unknowns for him not to worry. They'd been locked in a box for thirty-one days, and for twenty-three of those days, they didn't have their magic. If that wasn't bad enough in and of itself, up until the night before, they hadn't eaten for ten days, nine of which Kate was pregnant for.

He had two people to worry about now so he figured he had earned the right to worry, but he wouldn't harp on it. For now.

Hands still linked, they walked into the restaurant and were assaulted by the noise of voices. A crowd had already gathered, but the restaurant looked like it always had. Not a single decoration adorned the room to signal the holiday. Christmas had been the day before, but Isaac would never forget this day—December twenty-sixth—and not because it was the day after Christmas.

Thoughts of holidays were pushed to the back of his mind when Kate was pulled from his arms into a hug. Everyone wanted to hug them, to reassure themselves that he and Kate were alright. He understood, but it added up to a lot of hugs. As far as he could tell, almost everyone from the family dinners was present, even the people who didn't come every week. He guessed there were at least thirty people present.

To say it was overwhelming was putting it mildly. For over a month, it had been only him and Kate. He wanted that back, even for a few days, to give them time to adjust. Only minus the room in another dimension.

By the time the greetings were over and they'd found a place to sit, Meredith called everyone up to the buffet. Kate stood, and all Isaac wanted to do was whisk her back upstairs. Her cheeks were pale, and she didn't look as steady on her feet as she'd been earlier.

He was about to ask if he could go to the buffet for her when Fiona approached. With one hand on each of Kate's shoulders, she pushed her back into the chair.

Thank you, Isaac said to Fiona telepathically to not make a big deal out of her assistance. He expected his son's future grandmother would become an ally when he needed one, and it was never too early to take advantage of that.

"Let us fill plates for you," Fiona said as she lifted her chin toward where Morgana stood off to the side.

"Appreciate it." He smiled at them both before they walked away.

Kate leaned close and rubbed her hand over his bearded cheek. "I know what my mom just did, and for once, I don't mind. I'm okay, you know… yes, still weak. But okay."

"Are you feeling as overwhelmed as I am by all the people?" he asked quietly.

She laughed. "Yes, and I never thought I'd say that. I love these big get-togethers. But…" She looked over at the line of people at the buffet. "It's a lot today."

Kate admitting that something was almost too much was new for her. Usually, she would have been quick to state she could handle anything. And he knew she could, but she didn't need to, and it seemed she was finally coming to realize that.

"We can leave whenever you want to."

"I know." She stroked his beard with her palm again. "Are you going to keep this, my lumberjack?"

"Do you want me to?"

"Yes." Kate winked, something else that was new. "At least until I can come up with a new nickname."

"Just keep it family friendly," he teased. Keeping a beard was easy. Kate might not have realized it yet, but he would do anything for her, including keeping his beard.

A minute later, Fiona and Morgana brought over plates piled high with food. As he and Kate ate, they answered questions that were peppered at them.

"I'm sorry," Sam told them when there was a lull.

Isaac didn't know what she was sorry for, but he was familiar enough with the look of guilt to recognize it when he saw it. He'd seen it for years every time he looked in the mirror. "You don't have anything to be sorry for, Sam. Maverick is the only one to blame." Isaac noticed Mirek take one of Sam's hands and pull it under the table, as if to hold it in his lap. Maybe Isaac and Kate weren't the only ones who resolved some issues over the past month.

"Yes, but I told everyone you were dead." Her voice was strong and her stare direct, like she needed him to know she was taking responsibility for her actions.

Mirek looked as if he was going to speak up, so Isaac gave him a nod, hoping he realized that Isaac did not blame anyone but Maverick.

Mirek gave a slight nod in return for Isaac to continue. "Sam. Again... nothing to be sorry for. I expected Maverick made it seem like we were dead." Something he'd suspected from the beginning.

A chair scraped against the floor, drawing his attention. Ben stood, walked around to his daughter, and laid a hand on her shoulder, looking Isaac in the eyes. "We both thought you were dead. And I agree, it's on Maverick, but it pains me that we didn't find you sooner."

"Well, thank fuck you found us when you did!" Kate said loudly with a grin, breaking the tension as laughter broke out. Even Sam smiled, and Ben walked back to his chair now that his daughter seemed at ease. This time, Mirek nodded at Isaac.

"My sister has a way with words. And yes, we're thankful," Damon said when the laughter died down. "Since we were talking about Maverick... I'm curious about something with the room he sent you to... When did the walls start to collapse?"

Kate squeezed Isaac's hands, and he took that as a sign to take over. She kept a smile on her face, but his magic picked up on her emotional strain through their hands. "December first, the same day we lost our magic."

As soon as Isaac spoke, he felt the tension in the room return. There were subtle signs that confirmed his feeling. The clanking of cutlery on plates became quieter. A few of the council members locked eyes with their partners. Enough for Isaac to know that something else happened on December first.

Isaac looked down the tables at Jack. "Something else happened that day." Isaac didn't pose it as a question; he knew it in his gut.

"Yes. Maverick died," Jack said, his expression somber, telling Isaac that Maverick's death wasn't the worst thing to happen.

Kate's rising anxiety telegraphed to Isaac through her skin. Throwing his arm around her shoulders, he pulled her into his side, but Isaac's gaze remained on Jack. "And the ancient magic that was inside him?"

Jack's countenance changed, but only slightly, as if he'd been painted by a light brush. His expression held sorrow, and his shoulders appeared weighed down, but they didn't drop. "Unfortunately, it didn't stay inside him."

"It dissipated?" Kate asked.

"No, it escaped and infected others. It's been spreading."

Kate shifted, and Isaac saw her look around the tables as if taking a headcount. He understood the feeling of wanting to make sure everyone they knew was safe. "Yet our family and friends are all here... Ah... shit. That didn't come out right. I didn't mean it like that—other magics are important too—I'm just glad you all are here and alright." There were a few laughs amongst the group. "I meant to ask how you've all managed to stay safe."

Jack smirked. "It's okay, we all understand. And we're not sure if it's been any one thing we did. We closed the businesses, just like a lot of other magics have. We put stronger spells on the buildings that we reinforce every day, and everyone has the spell Reece first gave Isabella." Jack paused and turned to Reece. "You'll make sure Isaac and Kate have it?"

"Will do. Right after this."

"Good." Jack's gaze swung back to them. "We limit where we go, especially public places, although many of them are closed too. Authorities believe there is a widespread pandemic, and because only magics know of magic's existence, we're not about to reveal it just to reassure people that only magics are affected."

"It wouldn't work anyway. Once it's known that magic exists, it would open a whole new can of worms. And if it ever came out that at one time all people used to be magic and entire family lines lost magic over generations and their memories of magic with it, we could have multiple divides amongst both magics and non-magics," Ben interjected.

"True. Something we will avoid at all costs. Outing the existence of magic will never be an option," Jack continued. "Right now, we've got two things working on our side. One: no one but us knows that Maverick is dead. Thanks to Simon, we've been able to prevent that knowledge from getting out. Which leads to the second advantage. Thanks to Sam, we're working on a plan to contain the magic, and for that plan to work, we'll need everyone to believe that Maverick is alive. We can explain all that to you two later. What's more important right now is the sword."

Isaac felt Kate's anxiety turn to excitement. The feeling spilling into him took him by surprise. He'd never kept his magic flowing while touching someone before. Usually, he got what he needed and then pulled away, but not with Kate.

He was changing his rules for her. Trust had been the first rule to change when he'd trusted her to understand the risks and know what she could handle. Whereas in the past, he had only trusted himself to make all the decisions. Now it was his magic. With one arm draped around Kate's shoulder and the other holding her hand, Isaac's magic continued to monitor her emotions. It hadn't been a conscious decision on his part, but it felt like a natural progression as proof of their connection.

"Isaac gave me the tattoo," Kate announced. "I'm ready to work with the sword."

"Great," Jack said. "We'll let you rest today, but you should be strong enough to start tomorrow."

"Jack." Fiona's tone had all eyes turning to look at her. The last time Isaac heard her use that tone of voice was when she was putting Kate in her place. "Council leader or not, *you*," she said, emphasizing the pronoun, "do not get to make those decisions on your own. Kate is pregnant, and you will not put her in danger."

The matriarch of their group had spoken. Isaac felt something settle inside him, thankful he hadn't had to play the bad guy. Fiona was a formidable ally. And as long as Isaac stayed on her good side, he'd enjoy seeing her in that role.

"For fuck's sake, Fiona. I would never purposely put Kate in danger. We'll make sure Mirek is there to heal her—" Jack held up his hand to stall a protest from Fiona. "Just in case. I don't expect Mirek will be needed. We'll also have a contingent of guards. Again—just in case."

Jack turned in their direction. "Kate, Isaac. You both good with that?"

"All except for the waiting part," Kate said with a whine. "But I get it. Tomorrow morning at eight?"

"Sure. Mirek, that work for you?" After Mirek nodded, Jack addressed the group. "I heard Reece has dessert."

In all the years Isaac had known Jack, he'd never been overly fond of desserts. That probably hadn't changed, but the man had always been a good leader and knew when a diversion was needed. At his mention of dessert, conversations started up, and once more, the tension in the room dissipated.

If only dessert would be enough to ease Isaac's tension about Kate working with the sword.

22

Kate accepted a hug from her mom. "I'm okay, you know. I keep telling everyone that, but you wouldn't know it by the number of people here to babysit me." Kate smiled, hoping it took the edge off her words.

"Honey, I know you're alright. Everyone is just here as a precaution and to support you with the sword if it's needed."

Kate looked over to the large double doors of her workshop as Isaac was walked toward her. Sam and Mirek were there, along with Damon, Morgana, Simon, and Jo. A half-dozen of Jack and Ben's agents were standing off to the side.

"Hey, honey," her mom said as Isaac walked up, giving him a hug before continuing. "You have to remember that a lot happened to us too."

A bit of guilt nipped away at some of Kate's anticipation for the reason they were in her workshop. "I'm sorry, Mom. Even without all the details yet, I know from the

228

snippets I heard yesterday that you must have had some excitement."

Her mother gave an inelegant snort. "Excitement. Not the word I would use, but yes, we've been busy. Sam is the one who came up with the plan. And she was the one who figured out where you were once we knew you were alive. I thought…"

Her mom took in a big gulp of air and waved her hand in front of her face. Kate had seen her mom make that gesture to dry her tears many times over the years.

"I know we said we would explain what happened while you were in the room. And we will. But for now, you need to understand that for twenty-seven days, we thought you were dead. I couldn't—"

With sudden clarity, Kate realized what she'd said earlier, and interrupted her mom. "I'm so sorry. When I said you had some excitement, I wasn't thinking about that."

"I know what you meant, honey. It was a tough month, but after I had the vision, I realized you were both alive."

"Can you tell us about your vision, Fiona? I'd been sure I was dreaming until you told me to wake up," Isaac said as he put his arm around Kate. She leaned back into him, loving the feel of his closeness. She and Isaac hadn't been more than a few feet away from each other in the thirty-something hours since they were rescued. Kate expected that would change with time, but for now, she wasn't complaining.

"Sam and Ben were sure you died, they—" She waved her hand as if in dismissal. "Let them tell you about that later and how they found the other dimension. Anyway… Even though we were sure you were dead, I kept having the same vision about you lying on that white floor. Remember, the one I mentioned the day you touched the sword?"

Kate nodded, hoping her mom would get to how she was in Isaac's dream. She hadn't heard much about that yet.

"I think that vision is why I had trouble accepting that you were both dead and why I kept putting off the funeral."

"Oh my god!" Kate looked at Isaac. "I hadn't even thought about anyone holding funerals for us. Had you?"

He kissed her cheek. He didn't say anything, but she knew he'd had the thought.

"Fiona, how did you realize what the floor meant?" Isaac asked, turning the conversation away from their funerals.

"I didn't. At first, I had that vision every few days, but after we thought you had died, I had it at least once a day, although mostly at night. I'm not a truly gifted seer like some, but visions still feel different to me than dreams. I was becoming exhausted because I couldn't figure it out, and then on December twenty-first, I went to bed early. A few hours later, the same vision came to me. Then it changed. I saw Kate in the field behind this workshop, and she was with a little boy. I knew that little boy was my grandson."

"But how did you know?" Kate asked her mom.

"I just knew. I expect it's like the two of you with your special abilities—some things you just know."

"Fiona, how did you add me to your vision? I was dreaming and then the dream morphed into the vision. That's why I thought I was still dreaming."

"After I woke everyone up in the middle of the night..." Her mom paused to chuckle. "I told them I knew you were both alive because I had seen Kate's future son. Jack gathered everyone together, and it was Sam who figured out how to find you. Quantum entanglement something or other—she can explain it to you. We found you on Christmas Eve, but we couldn't get inside the room, and we couldn't reach you. We needed your help to break through the wall."

"But Jack spoke to me telepathically."

"That was after. He and Meredith tried to get through to both of you for over an hour, but you never answered."

"I'm guessing that had something to do with how Maverick set up the room. I'm curious, but someone can explain that later too. I think there's a lot we'll want to hear about, but for now, tell us how you brought me into your vision."

Her mom practically beamed. "Reece figured out that one. He'd come across a spell that allows a dreamer to enter a vision. It took me three tries, but then you heard me. Once you left the vision, I figured you had woken up. That's when Jack reached out to you... and you know the rest."

"Can I see the vision?" Kate asked.

"I don't see why not. We can try—"

Jack appeared with a wrapped bundle in his arms, cutting off her mom.

She pulled away from Isaac to hug her mom and whisper in her ear. "Thank you for not giving up on us. Can you show me the vision later?"

"Of course, honey," her mom whispered back, tears in her voice.

Kate was as curious as Isaac about everything that had happened while they'd been in the room, but she would worry about it all later. Right now, she wanted to touch the sword. To see if Isaac's tattoo made a difference.

"Kate, you want this on your bench?" Jack asked, already moving toward it.

She didn't give Jack an answer since he didn't need one.

Jack laid the bundle on Kate's workbench and turned toward her and Isaac. "I've got other business, so I'm not going to stay. Isaac, you'll reach out if you need me?"

"Of course. But Kate's got this."

Her pride swelled at the feeling of trust Isaac had in her. "Yeah, I've got this," Kate told Jack, and he nodded before flashing away.

Isaac placed his hands on her upper arms, turning her toward him. "If something happens, I'm going to put my hands on you to feel your emotions. It's not that I don't trust you to do your job. It's because we're dealing with ancient magic and the unknown, okay?"

She leaned forward and brushed his lips lightly with hers. "You can put your hands on me anytime, my lumberjack."

He chuckled and pulled back. "Glad to hear it. Now I'll let you get to work."

Unlike last time, the bundle wasn't held together with rope. Using her magic, she flicked the cloth aside to reveal the sword and took in the sight. She felt the same sense of awe she'd had the first time she'd seen it. The sword was a masterpiece.

Even though touching the blade hadn't gone well the last time, she knew this time would be different. Doing exactly what she'd done before, she touched the blade with the tips of all eight fingers at once.

Just like before, a pulse of energy shot up her arms, jerking her shoulders while her fingers stayed on the blade. The feelings in the blade settled down, sending a soothing current through her fingers and she knew for sure this time would be different.

She closed her eyes and relaxed her fingers as she listened to the blade tell her that all the stories passed down about how to contain the evil magic were wrong.

Isaac sensed the moment Kate went into a trance. He'd been prepared but had held out hope that it wouldn't happen.

"We have to stop her," Fiona said, walking toward Kate. "It's like when she touched it the first time. She lost over six hours."

"No, don't touch her," he said, circling his fingers around Fiona's wrist to prevent her from getting to Kate.

"Can't you see what it's doing to her?" Fiona demanded as she tried to wrench out of Isaac's clasp. He added some magic to his grip in a move that surprised him at how instinctively he'd done it.

They both knew Fiona could have added her own magic to the mix and forced him to let go. Instead, she stilled and looked him in the eyes. "You don't think she's in trouble?"

Isaac released Fiona but didn't apologize for detaining her. "No, I don't, but I will monitor her. I told Kate that if this happened, I'd use my magic to read her emotions." He took a step toward Kate and stopped, looking over his shoulder at Fiona. "I won't pull her away unless I think she or the baby are in trouble. I have to trust her."

"You're right." Fiona huffed out a dry laugh. "Please be patient with me. For almost a month, I believed you were both dead. I'm going to be a bit overprotective for a while."

"Understood."

Fiona had asked him to be patient with her, and now he had to give that to Kate. Calling on every ounce of patience he possessed, a skill he'd been honing since being with Kate, he walked up behind her.

Leaving only a few inches between their bodies, he placed his hands on her hips and let his magic out. Closing his eyes, he pushed his magic to reach for her emotions.

He felt an immediate pushback and breathed a sigh of relief—Kate was fine. Her magic didn't tell him in words, only feelings, but he sensed the pushback was reassurance.

Sliding his right hand from her hip around to her stomach, he spread it across her belly. The feeling was of pure warmth. Although he didn't sense a heartbeat, he knew it was there, and it wouldn't be that many weeks before he would be able to sense one.

Their magic had forged a bond. There was no way to know if it was because of the magic he'd embedded in her tattoos or because of their love, but there was no denying it was there.

Keeping one hand on Kate's hip and the other on her belly, he let the minutes tick by. As long as both mom and baby were doing okay, he'd trust Kate to get the information she needed.

Every few minutes, her magic pushed back, letting him know she was still aware of what was going on around her. That was enough for him.

"Isaac?" Fiona asked, her voice laced with worry.

He turned his head to look at Fiona. "Kate's fine. As is the baby. I can feel them both."

"What if she's in the trance for hours?"

"I don't think she's in a trance. It's my guess that she's talking to the sword. And if that's true, she'll probably be finished soon." He laughed at his own words. "I mean… how much can a sword have to say?"

It was clear Fiona didn't appreciate his joke, but Isaac was going to trust Kate.

He glanced at the clock on the wall. Thirty minutes had passed since she'd laid her fingers on the sword. Until Isaac felt something was off with either Kate or the baby, he would continue to wait.

True to his word to Fiona, the sword must have run out of things to say because five minutes later, Kate was finished.

She spun in his hands, but he didn't let go until he'd kissed her. Since they weren't alone in her workshop, the kiss wasn't long or deep, but it was enough for the moment.

"We were wrong," she said, grinning from ear to ear. "We don't need a lock."

"Then what do we need?" Sam asked, walking up with Mirek, Damon, Morgana, Jo, and Simon.

"The sword, which we have." Her expression sobered. "Unfortunately, we need an ancient spellbook too. I can sketch some details of it because I saw it in my mind, but I don't know where it is."

"Well, that's handy," Simon said. "We found a spellbook and didn't know what it was for, only that a spell we were using said we would need the book."

Isaac had so many questions he wanted to ask, but he expected them finding the book was another one of those things that happened while he and Kate were in the room. Like everything else they wanted to know, they'd learn about it sooner or later.

Mirek turned to Kate, a small smile on his face. "I'm glad you didn't need my services today."

A laugh of relief burst from Kate. "Me too. Now, we—"

An FBI agent landed inside the workshop less than five feet away. "Protect yourselves!" he shouted. "We're under attack!"

23

"For fuck's sake!" Kate muttered. She was getting really sick and tired of being attacked. Especially at her shop.

"Kate, flash to my apartment," Isaac ordered.

"I need to get the sword." She turned toward her workbench as a large crash, like metal on metal, resonated through the building.

Spinning back around, she saw men storm into her shop. One of her large workshop doors rocked back and forth on the floor, the hinges torn from its frame.

Kate started to count the number of men coming at them but lost track at ten as they continued to flood in. They numbered maybe fifteen or twenty, outnumbering their group, even with the FBI agents.

"I've contacted, Jack," Damon yelled over the sound of stomping boots and the men calling to each other as they came toward them.

"Throw up shields," Jack commanded as he landed amongst their group.

"We need Reece too," Sam shouted.

"Here," Reece declared from where he landed beside Jack.

Kate threw up a protective shield around herself. She felt like an idiot, realizing she could have done the same thing at the restaurant with Isabella. If she'd done it before they had grabbed her, she wouldn't have been hurt that night.

"Kate, get the sword and leave," Isaac demanded.

Isaac was right to tell Kate to leave. She needed to protect the sword because she was the only one who could, but she was also the only one pregnant with his child. He hadn't said it because he didn't need to. He was right; she needed to leave. For both reasons.

"Look who we have here," a voice bellowed from the front of her shop. She looked up to see Crouching Man from the restaurant walk toward the front of his group of minions. "It's the bitch from the restaurant," he told the group.

"Holy fuck," she whispered under her breath. Beside Crouching Man was the other guy from the restaurant, but that wasn't what shocked her. Her astonishment came from seeing two of the restaurant's patrons standing in front of her as mind-controlled minions. That could have been her and Isabella.

A hush fell over the room like a calm before the storm. Both groups stood, facing off.

She wanted to stay and help, but she also wanted to protect her unborn child and the sword. It was an easy decision.

But to get the sword, she'd have to drop her protection.

"I'm leaving," she said loudly enough for Isaac and Jack to hear. Telepathy wouldn't work with her shield up, and she wouldn't drop her protection until the last moment.

"Good, you're useless to us," Jack said equally as loud.

Kate froze—she knew Jack's comment was to aid her escape, but his words felt no different than the taunts from her past.

Like snapshots flashing before her eyes, she could see Brandon at the prom saying he didn't need her anymore, that he'd gotten what he wanted. Then Justin calling her a cold-hearted bitch. Finally, Ethan asking for his engagement ring back and saying she couldn't cut it.

To all three of them, she had become useless. They had used her until they got what they wanted and then discarded her.

"Kate."

She looked up at the sound of Isaac's voice. He brought her back to the present and made her remember what mattered most. *I love you with everything that I am.* The guys in her past didn't matter.

At one time, she would have needed to stay and prove herself, but not anymore.

"Fuck you, I'm leaving!" she yelled, putting as much defiance in her voice as she could. She dropped the shield and flashed to her workbench.

As she reached for the sword, someone yanked on her hair, cranking her head backward. Kate closed her fingers around the sword as she was pulled away from her bench.

When the grip on her hair loosened, she pivoted on her heels and assumed a fighting stance. The sword became an extension of her arm, the tip of the blade touching Crouching Man's Adam's apple, ready to slice him open.

"Think you're tough, don't you, bitch?" he taunted.

"I don't *think* it. I know it. And you need a bigger vocabulary. How about you—" Kate flashed to Isaac's apartment, the sword still in her hand. She'd purposely left her sentence unfinished so the idiot wouldn't anticipate her next move.

"And that's because I'm a badass," she whispered to herself.

"Yes, you are," Isaac said from behind her.

Startled, she spun around. "You're here!" She took a step forward and laughed at herself because she was still holding the sword. Using her magic, she propelled the sword to lay it on the counter but didn't wait for it to land. She jumped into Isaac's arms, knowing he'd catch her.

Holding her tight and with her legs wrapped around him, he walked over to the couch and sank down. Straddling his lap, Kate pressed her hands on his cheeks, loving the feel of his beard against her palms. "I love you, my lumberjack."

"I love you too."

She leaned in for a kiss and then pulled back. "Wait. You're here!"

"I think we established that," he said with a laugh and leaned forward to kiss her.

Putting a hand to his chest, she paused his movement. "Funny man. That's not what I meant... I meant, why aren't you at my workshop? Why didn't you stay to help the others? Are they okay? What about my shop? Are Maverick's minions still there? Don't they need you?" The questions came tumbling out of her one after the other as they popped into her head.

Isaac laid his fingers on her lips to stop any further verbal vomiting. "Everything is going to be okay. Sam mentioned this morning that she expected some of Maverick's people had probably been watching your shop since the day we disappeared. Sam said she warned the council to be prepared for an attack, and they decided that if one occurred, they'd use it as a test run for extracting and containing the evil magic. Because of that, I'm sure everyone is fine. And just as Jack was telling me to leave, Meredith, Isabella, Ben, Frank, Rowena, Connor, and a couple of others arrived. Between them all, the infected magics don't stand a chance. And I'm sure your shop will be fine too."

A sense of relief washed over Kate. "What do we do now? Wait?"

"I'm sure Jack will call us when they're finished at your shop and tell us where to meet so we talk about what's next. So until then… yes, we wait. Any ideas on how we can fill the time?"

"I'm sure I can think of something," she said just before her lips covered his.

It took only seconds for their kiss to explode, turning white-hot.

When his lips finally left hers, she felt bereft, craving his touch. She leaned forward to kiss him again when a cool breeze hit her skin.

She laughed but wouldn't complain that they were both naked, their clothes probably in a tidy pile some- where. Being skin to skin with Isaac felt right. They'd spent so much time just like this while in the room. The feeling of him between her legs became heated, and she ground her pelvis into his.

The sudden rush to have him inside her mellowed. Kate still wanted to feel him sink into her, to fill her up. That hadn't lessened, just the urgency. First, she wanted to give back to Isaac.

Slowing their kisses, she savored his mouth before moving down to his jaw. Running her fingers through the thick growth of beard, she tugged lightly, feeling him swell where she straddled him.

Moving lower still, her hands followed her lips. She took one nipple into her mouth, biting it softly, then blew on the hardened nub. Isaac groaned and his fingers weaved into her hair.

When she gave his other nipple the same attention, his fingers wound tighter into her hair. The sharp tug of pain sent jolts of electricity through her core. She grew wetter with each tug.

Slipping off his lap, she kneeled between his legs and braced her hands on his thighs. Leaning forward, she ran her tongue along his cock from base to tip. It jerked at her touch, and he groaned.

Pleasing him was a heady feeling. It made her feel both loved and powerful. She licked him again, his thigh muscles tensing beneath her palms.

Her hair fell forward, and before she could push it out of the way, Isaac grabbed a large section, wrapping it around his fist. Kate moaned at the exquisite stimulation.

"Let me fuck your mouth," he whispered.

Looking up with just her eyes, she watched him stroke himself several times. Then she let her eyes drift closed as he fed her his cock. Closing her lips around him, she sucked as he thrust his hips forward. His fists tightened in her hair again, and she lost herself in the sensations. The tug on her scalp, the growing heat pooling between her legs, and the feel of Isaac's dick tunneling in and out of her mouth as he groaned was almost enough to send her over the edge all on their own.

He pulled back, her mouth leaving him with a wet pop. "What's wrong?"

"Absolutely nothing! Your mouth is amazing, but I just want to feel you around me when I come." Reaching down, he lifted her back onto his lap.

Straddling Isaac again, Kate held onto his shoulders and positioned her feet flat on the cushions. When she lifted up several inches, Isaac entered her in one fluid motion.

"Yes!" she grunted as her body acclimated to the delicious fullness. Using his shoulders for leverage, she hovered above him as he punched up into her. It quickly became fierce and carnal—an exquisite exchange of give and take. She rocked against him as he drove up deep into her, taking them closer and closer.

"Oh, fuck," she cried out as her body tightened and the pleasure rushed up quickly, shredding her as she exploded. Isaac drove up into her several more times and then called out her name as he found his own release.

They didn't move for several minutes, wrapped in each other's arms as their breathing returned to normal. When he slipped out of her, she was too sated to care.

A moment later, Isaac thrust to his feet with her in his arms, magic obviously powering his legs. She wrapped her own legs around his waist, her head still against his chest, as he walked to the bathroom.

"We'll shower and then we'll reach out to Jack to find out when and where to meet. Since it's close to lunch time, we'll probably meet at The Magic Plate, but I'll check." He lowered her feet to the floor. "You okay, Turquoise?"

"I'm more than okay. And I'm excited to fill everyone in on what the sword told me."

She was nervous about what it told her needed to happen next and wasn't sure they'd be able to pull it off.

$\mathcal{K}$ate shut the apartment door, the envelope clutched in her hand.

"Was that Jack I heard?" Isaac asked as he came down the hall from the bedrooms.

"Yes. At lunch, I asked him if he'd go to my shop to get something for me. I figured he'd be fast and it would be safest for him."

Taking her free hand, Isaac tugged her over to the couch. "Come sit with me."

Gently prying the envelope from her fingers, he tossed it on the coffee table with a casual, "Later."

Sitting, he tugged her down almost on top of him. They laughed, and she shifted to straddle his lap. Cupping his bearded cheeks in her hands, she leaned in for a kiss. "I like this position."

"I like it too."

Their kiss was slow, not the passion that had driven them earlier in the afternoon.

"We're missing something." He leaned to the side to look around her.

"What are you up to?"

He pulled the coffee table closer and put his feet on it so his legs were bent. "I realized we have four positions…" He held up his fingers and ticked them off. "One is spooning. Two is side to side, your hand on my chest. Number three and four are this one."

Kate leaned back against Isaac's thighs like she'd done so many times on their cramped bed in the room. He put his hand in hers, the gesture so familiar it settled something inside her.

"I'm guessing the second variation of this position is the one where we're naked? Like we did before lunch?"

"Exactly. But if you need a refresher, I'd be happy to demonstrate again later."

She gave him an exaggerated wink. "I'll hold you to it!"

They were silent for a while, something they'd become so comfortable with in the last month.

When Isaac finally spoke, she could tell that he was worried. He had a small crease between his eyes, and his fingers gave hers another squeeze. Their silent form of communication.

"It's only been forty-eight hours since we were rescued… and a lot has happened since then." He leaned forward and kissed her softly on the lips. Just a brushing. A reassurance. "I don't think we've even begun to process what we went through in the last month, but we've got time. I think there's something else, though. I can almost feel your gears turning. Talk to me, Kate."

Her thumb glided along Isaac's palm. In such a short time, this innocent touch had become her safety net.

She thought back to that morning when her fingers touched the sword. "When the sword spoke to me this morning… it's hard to explain… I felt a sense of pride, but it was more than that. Well… first… talking to a sword was a bit strange, even for us." She laughed as she remembered her surprise and excitement. "But then, it was like I was being trusted with the most powerful gift." Looking into Isaac's light-gray eyes, she saw his love and acceptance, and his trust too. "With your tattoo, you made that happen."

"No, Turquoise, you made it happen. The tattoo I gave you was just a tool to assist you." His lips curved up in a small smile. "Since we're already talking swords, maybe this won't seem so strange… But I think the sword trusted you. It killed Isabella's brother, knocked your mentor out, and disguised itself to non-magics, but it tried to communicate with you. From the first time you touched it, it knew it could trust you. You just needed a way to communicate with it—the tattoo gave you that."

Kate linked her hands with both of his. "You make me feel like I'm enough," she whispered.

"You are. You always have been. Maybe just too stubborn to see it," he teased.

"Hey, I thought I was assertive."

"Yes, that too."

She gave him a mock elbow to the stomach, then leaned against him, her head on his chest, their arms going around each other.

"Are you good with what was discussed at lunch?" he asked after a few minutes of just holding each other.

When she sat back to see Isaac's face, he put his hand in hers. She'd never imagined a man giving her the kind of love and trust that Isaac did. A familiar burning formed in her throat—the formation of happy tears. She swallowed to push them back, because happy or not, she didn't want to cry.

She thought about Isaac's question. "Yes. When everyone is ready, I'll take the sword and lock in the magic."

"And you'll let me touch you like I did today?"

"You can touch me anytime, my lumberjack."

"I believe you said those same words this morning." He squeezed her fingers and then his smile disappeared. "When I touched you this morning... and felt both you and our baby... knowing you were both alright... it was like nothing I'd ever felt before. I think you forged us together with our love."

Kate laughed. "Oh man, my lumberjack. That's your corniest line yet. But I love it, and I love you." More than she could ever express.

They'd almost lost each other, but now they had a second chance. She just had to believe Sam's plan would work. "It's hard to imagine that by tomorrow night or the night after, the evil magic could be gone for good." It seemed too easy, although she knew that none of what they'd all gone through was easy.

Sam had told them at lunch that the test run of extracting the evil magic they'd done at her shop was successful. Now Damon and Simon were doing their thing, and then it was Kate's turn.

"I hope Damon and Simon are okay. It sounded dangerous." After everything they'd been through in the last couple of years, she needed the drama to be over and for her family and friends to finally be safe once and for all.

"They'll be fine. We have to trust that they wouldn't have volunteered if they didn't think they could handle it. And since we've got a bit of time before they need us…" He held out his hand, and the envelope floated over from the coffee table.

When she took it from him, it seemed so crazy now. For years, she'd let the experiences linked to the items in the envelope stop her from finding happiness.

The edges of the envelope were creased from being stuffed into the drawer, its surface strewn with black smudges. Nothing remarkable—just an ordinary, old envelope. Yet she'd let it hold power over her.

As if sensing what she needed, Isaac held out his hands between them, palms up. Upending the envelope, she dumped the items into his hands.

Isaac looked at the items and then at her. "I think we need to add one more item."

"No, these are from the assholes who hurt me."

"I know. Hold open the envelope, please." When she had the envelope open wide, Isaac dumped the items inside. Then he conjured an empty water bottle and put it inside the envelope. Next, he conjured a wide piece of tape and sealed it shut.

Kate frowned in confusion. "I don't get it. Why did you put an empty water bottle in there?"

"Because everything that was in that envelope is from men who have hurt you. But not all men are like that." He tossed the envelope on the coffee table and wrapped his hand around the back of her neck.

"I would never intentionally hurt you, so that empty water bottle represents me." She felt Isaac's magic seeping from his palm, right over the tattoo he'd inked on her neck. "Kate, I love you so much that I would give you my last drop of water." He kissed her softly, and this time a happy tear fell, but Isaac caught it with his thumb.

"I love you, my lumberjack."

"I know." His grin made her laugh.

"Since we have some time before we have to help save the world… let's call my mom so she can show me her vision. Then how about we start picking baby names? It might be early for non-magic couples, but you've already seen our son as a toddler."

"I would love that, Turquoise. Then later we can try out the other variation of this position," Isaac said as he wiggled his eyebrows.

She laughed again. For now, all was right with their world. In the worst of circumstances, she and Isaac had forged a love unlike any she'd ever thought possible. Their future was bright, but not just hers and Isaac's. There was finally hope ahead for all magics.

MIREK STOOD at the back of The Magic Plate, leaning against the wall, his hands shoved in the front pockets of his jeans. To anyone watching, he would look relaxed. Not carefree, per se, but not angry or impatient either. Like he was hanging around waiting for what was going to happen next.

He'd perfected the pose years ago. So often, his magic had been drained, and without it to cool off his anger and frustration from the atrocities he'd seen, he had learned self-preservation meant presenting a carefree attitude.

His captors hadn't hidden their hatred for their charges, even while using them. That had taught Mirek early on that eliciting strong emotion or defying an order resulted in punishment. He would have withstood any torture they had wanted to inflict upon him to protect the others. But his captors knew that.

To keep Mirek in line, Sam had become their target.

Mirek let his gaze wander around the restaurant until it settled on Sam. She was talking with her dad. If Mirek had been stronger, Sam might not have been separated from her family for more than twenty years.

He had failed her, in so many ways. But she wasn't the only one he had failed, and some mistakes could never be fixed.

Tonight, if Mirek could convince Sam to alter her plan to contain the evil magic, maybe he wouldn't fail her again.

Sam looked up at her uncle, the action causing her hair to fall backward over her shoulder. Even from where Mirek stood across the room, he could see the burn scars on the right side of Sam's face that trailed down her neck and onto her shoulder.

He counted down the seconds… Three, two, one… and then Sam's hand came up, pulling her hair forward to cover her right side.

For years, he had tried to break her of the habit. She didn't need to hide.

Even with the scars, she was the most beautiful woman he'd ever met. He would never be able to convince her of that, although he'd tried for years. She'd been his entire world since he was ten years old, and he would do anything for her.

When Mirek looked at her, he didn't see the scars. He saw her beauty, both what was on the inside and the outside. He saw intelligence, strength, kindness, loyalty, and most of all, the innocence she'd somehow managed to maintain in the face of all the horrors they'd seen.

No, he didn't focus on her scars, but he couldn't forget they were there because to him, they represented more than just what she'd been through. They also represented how he had failed her time and again for over twenty years.

Now Mirek worried he would fail her again because six years ago, he'd made her a promise. If he kept that promise… in two days, Sam would be dead.

Thanks so much for reading *Forged in Magic!*
NEXT IN THE IN MAGIC SERIES:
With dark forces closing in, Sam and Mirek must face the secrets of their pasts and find the courage to believe in their love, or magic as they know it will be lost forever in
FOREVER IN MAGIC
https://books2read.com/forever-in-magic

ALSO BY KJ WARAWA

IN MAGIC SERIES

Lost in Magic

Truth in Magic

Found in Magic

Courage in Magic

Love in Magic

Forged in Magic

Forever in Magic

CURSED TO LOVE SERIES

Cursed to Love

Cursed to Dream

ABOUT KJ WARAWA

Paranormal romance author KJ Warawa had worked every job under the sun, including swimwear seller, switchboard operator, legal secretary, sign language interpreter, soldier, massage therapist, and process improvement advisor, before settling into the career she'd always dreamed about: Author.

She still loves processes and spreadsheets, doesn't love massaging feet, and is currently living out her own love story in Alberta, Canada.

STAY IN TOUCH WITH KJ:
Join KJ's Newsletter at
https://kjwarawa.com/free-book/
to receive a FREE book, exclusive deals, special offers, behind-the-scenes info, and learn about new releases, plus more!
www.kjwarawa.com